A Horse of Another Color

ILLINOIS SHORT FICTION

A Horse of Another Color

Stories by
Carolyn Osborn

UNIVERSITY OF ILLINOIS PRESS

Urbana   Chicago   London

"The Apex Man," *Red Clay Reader,* no. 3, 1966.

"The Vulture Descending Each Day," *Texas Quarterly,* Winter, 1968.

"My Brother Is a Cowboy," *Roanoke Review,* Spring, 1970.

"G T T," *Descant,* Spring, 1972.

"A Miniature Folly," *Four Quarters,* Summer, 1973.

"In Captivity," *Aphra,* Winter, 1975.

"The Accidental Trip to Jamaica," *Antioch Review,* Winter, 1977.

Library of Congress Cataloging in Publication Data

Osborn, Carolyn, 1934–
  A horse of another color.

  (Illinois short fiction)
  I. Title.
PZ4.07678Ho   [PS3565.S348]   813'.5'4   77-21724
ISBN 0–252–00671–2
ISBN 0–252–00672–0 pbk.

For Joe

Contents

A Miniature Folly

Three long rowboats full of men came steadily up the Thames to Westminster Pier. Each boat flew a flag so heavy it dragged the water. Alice Richards, waiting on the pier for a barge to leave for Hampton Court, squinted at the flags trying to distinguish letters and coats of arms. The sparkle of sun on water combined with a high wind rippling the material made it impossible for her to see complete designs. As they came closer, she saw all the men wore white trousers although each crew wore different-colored sweaters. No one surrounding her, not even the English tourists, could tell her who the rowers were, nor what they were doing on the river in July.

"Some kind of ceremony, I suppose," was the only answer she got to her questions, one which failed to satisfy her, but apparently satisfied the English woman who gave it. Their lives, she felt with the quick envy of an American abroad, were full of ceremony, while hers was lacking. Since Sunday she'd been thinking it was not only that her life was lacking the richness of ceremony, but that she was also deficient in another way. Twice she'd been followed. At thirty-six she was still attractive, a slender woman with good legs, dark red hair, and eyes her husband described as "flaming blue." Men turned to look at her, which was pleasant.

The ones who'd followed her lately, however, were not pleasant. Little, short men with strange looks in their eyes were attracted to her. At the National Portrait Gallery she was surprised to see herself framed in a mirror among all the famous heads. The gallery's director was evidently aware of visitors' loss of identity when continually studying other people's faces. With the mirror she was reminded, these are only people marked by history; you are marked by your own, and if you are not immortalized by fame, here is your moment. Just between her head and shoulders, a small, moon-faced man smiled. Keeping one obsequious step behind her, he accompanied her to every room, commenting on every portrait she paused before. She refused him a word until she could stand no more. In a doorway where a guard waited she turned to face her pursuer and quietly said, "Go away, please." She waited with the guard until he was gone. Coming out of the Victoria and Albert yesterday a stooped old man, his lips twisted in a contorted grin, had passed her on the side-walk, waited until she'd passed him, then had positively chased her into a cab. Alice shuddered at the memory.

Where did they come from . . . these sad, ugly people . . . what within her drew them? There are many beautiful women in London, and she was not that startling a beauty. Though she had friends living there, she was frequently alone. Was that what beckoned them . . . one solitary shining before another? She disliked her loneliness, felt it almost a stigma, but her husband couldn't come to Europe with her every time and her friends couldn't be expected to accompany her to every museum. To have men glance her way, to be appreciated, was one thing, to attract peculiar men was another.

She sighed and wondered if she looked older, more appealing to freaks, and at the same moment self-consciously regarded herself a fool for falling into the tiresome attitude of a woman worrying about her age. One of the more irritating things about traveling alone was the chance of discovering appalling truths about oneself. At home, Alice reassured herself, she had a handsome husband. They'd produced two beautiful children and if there was anything fatally strange about her, she wished she knew what it was! She wished just once she'd be followed by a majestic male, an Adonis, instead of the reprehensible little men who had been slinking around after her.

She sat down on a bench and pulled her coat collar up around her face. The boat should be taking off soon. What were they waiting for? Behind her she heard men's voices. The crews from the rowboats were tying them on back and climbing aboard the barge. They seemed to be every age, though none were terribly young and three wearing jackets were definitely hearty old men.

A man in a crimson sweater called to someone he knew up front, "Jerry, we'll be pushing off now." He and all his mates immediately disappeared into the saloon bar below deck. Jerry, standing on the pier, was just the sort who never followed her—tall, blonde, vigorous-looking, well-muscled without being a muscle-man, handsome without being effete, and sure of himself. Looking over the boatload of tourists, he uncoiled the last loop of rope as he leaped on board. They slid under Westminster Bridge and past the Houses of Parliament. Alice gave up worrying about who followed her and began discovering London from the river. Should she take a picture of Parliament again? Ridiculous! She already had innumerable pictures taken on other trips, but this was the famous side, wasn't it? Must I always have the famous side? Compulsive photographer! Compulsive tourist! She took the picture, sat down and watched while wharves, piles of lumber, and the industrial underpinnings of the city quickly gave way to green banks and boat houses.

A rich bellow of singing male voices rolled up the stairway from the saloon. Alice said to the woman at the end of her bench, "I wonder who they are?"

The woman gave her a shrug which dismissed singers or any curiosity about anything. Alice found out she was an American from Chicago who had gotten tired of her tour and gone off for a whole day on her own. Unfortunately, she was lost on her own. She'd made arrangements to get to Hampton Court, but none at all for returning to London. Any interest she'd ever had was killed by anxiety. Of course she could return by the same boat, Alice suggested.

"Yes," the woman sighed. She had a lot of hair stuffed under a close-fitting hat and her eyebrows had been plucked in two fine, arched lines, yet the other lines of her face drew together in a series of shrewd wrinkles. Her appearance would have allowed her the role of a sybil, but she couldn't play up to it. "This boat," she moaned, "it takes forever and I go to the theatre tonight."

What sort of accent did she have? "Are you Italian?" asked Alice, who had an immense curiosity. She would eventually furnish the woman information about trains to London from Hampton Court, but before she did she intended to find out a few things. Despite her prophetess face, the woman, who was of Italian descent, turned out to be a lady interested only in pleasantries concerning the beauty of the landscape.

Alice was not at all intrigued by a running murmur of "Oh, how beautiful . . . lovely . . . Did you ever see such trees?" She preferred talking to people who could tell her something she did not know, people wiser than she, or those who were personally compelling. If she couldn't find one of this sort, she preferred silence. Bored by the Italian lady, she went below deck and ordered a half pint of bitter and a sandwich. It was a small place with stairs at one end, bar at the other, seats and tables against the walls, and it was full of men. Earlier she would have been timid; after two weeks in London she'd gotten used to walking into pubs by herself. No one would annoy her, or even try to start a conversation, but if she chose to she could. Never before had she chosen, but this time it was only natural to talk to a tall, white-haired man.

"Would you tell me, please, what you are all doing here?"

"It's Swan-Upping Day."

"What?" The roar of voices and beat of the engine drowned out his reply.

"Come over here, dear." He led her to a table where everyone was dressed in crimson sweaters.

"You're an American, aren't you?"

Alice nodded. She would not mention she was from Texas as she'd learned the English were fascinated by the mere size of the state as well as the cowboy myth. It took too long to disillusion them, and all efforts to do so were useless. Since she'd been abroad for several summers, she'd adjusted to the needs of Europeans. There really should be a place like the mythical Texas, a distant place where evil was overcome daily by men six feet tall, where either oil or cattle made everyone rich and vast spaces were open for new beginnings. The fact that it didn't exist was not important. Europeans knew that, joked about the clichés, yet still hungered for them. And all the time she was among them, wasn't she searching for corroborations of her particular illusions, insisting on Camelot when it couldn't be found?

"What happens on Swan-Upping Day?"

"It's this way. We're going up the river to catch some swans and band them for the Queen. Royal bird, you know. We're the Queen's Lightermen. We all work at the port."

"Like our longshoremen?"

"I suppose."

Language barrier. She was forever running into one. As usual Alice was frustrated over her inability to translate exactly.

"And the others?"

"The ones in the blue sweaters are the vintners, and those in white are the dyers. Guilds, you know."

"I thought swans were the Queen's birds."

"They are, have been since the days of Henry the Eighth when he had to save them from the poachers. The guilds also got the privilege. The vintners make two cuts in the beaks, the dyers, one. They rub a bit of tar in to let the necks be seen." He leaned forward, smiling, enjoying his explanation.

Alice smiled back. She couldn't have been more delighted.

"The female is called a pen and the male, a cob. They mate for life."

"Like people," said Alice. Looking down at her hands she noticed the diamond in her engagement ring. Gross? Two carats. It had been her grandmother's. Gross or not, she liked it.

"Yes. Umm." He laughed. "You're married, aren't you. Have another half pint, dear?"

"Oh, no, thank you. It makes me drunk."

"Does us all. I'm a little bit myself right now. Beg your pardon for anything I've done—"

"You haven't done anything." How could he think he'd been offensive? Oh, the English and their dreadful reserve! They were so often afraid of breaking down and becoming monsters! He acted as if there was a tiny round mirror at the bottom of his stein where he'd see his cheerful face transformed into a gargoyle glare.

"My name's Ned. Used to own a pub down in Southampton. Listened to the public talk all the time. Now I do the talking."

"Is it hard to catch the swans?"

"The old cobs can be tough—thrashing about in the water while you try to upend them."

"Only if you're an old cob yourself!"

Alice jerked her head up to face the young man who'd been standing on the pier.

"Go on, Ned, give the rest of us a chance."

"Get us another pint, won't you, Jerry?" Ned shoved the stein toward him.

"Only if you'll give up your seat when I get back."

"I'll not."

"It's unfair to keep her all to yourself."

"What's fair play got to do with it?"

Jerry leaned across Ned's back. "This old fellow will be deserting you at the locks. Will you have a drink with me then?"

"All right." Alice, embarrassed by the effects of wishful thinking, could barely look at him. He was only a boy . . . he couldn't have known her thoughts. Surely he'd been too far away to pick her out of the crowd sitting on the barge.

All three crews left at the next set of locks. Alice took their pictures as they clambered unsteadily into their boats. A slight breeze unfurled a flag behind Ned, flattened it so she could easily read the crimson letters E.R. on a white background and, above them, a crown.

The day, still bright and clear, was turning out to be ridiculously romantic, yet she wasn't fool enough to believe she'd stepped into the past. Henry the Eighth, swan-upping, royal birds, Queen's Lightermen in crimson and white were all very well; on the same barge there were at least twenty-five black school children on a field trip, a bewildered Italian-American lady, and a sour-faced Englishman who voiced his disapproval.

"Ah, they're all off getting drunk. Taking the day off, larking. Nothing but an excuse for boozing. They'll spend the night in some duke's house and spend the rest of the year telling how grand it was."

"They'll spend all day chasing swans in rowboats," said Alice, who felt the men in all three crews were marvelously robust, decent fellows.

"Their wings are clipped." The sour-faced man scratched his forehead irritably as though something itched, but he didn't know quite what.

"They'll still have to catch them and band their legs, nick the beaks."

"No." The man shook his head.

"You don't think they really—"

He shook his head again.

Alice subsided and shook her own inwardly. There was nothing to be done with such a skeptic . . . nasty sort . . . all too willing to condemn others for having a good time.

The swan-uppers' boats were a patch of orange against blue, then gone. There were more small houses on stilts on the banks now, doors at water level for boats, living space above outlined in white balustrades. Although they had a purpose, the boat houses appeared to be miniature follies surrounded by gardens. In front of one three small boys were trying to paddle a blue and white boat in three directions. Alice, thinking of her own children living in Texas, which seemed more arid than usual at the moment, regretted they'd never have the casual pleasure of messing about in boats. Untrue, she warned herself, completely untrue. There was a lake only blocks from her house . . . man-made, yes, created by bulldozers, yes, but water. And there were houses all around it, some just as fanciful as those by the Thames, more so as they were larger and more expensive. The comparison failed. The lake she knew was artificial, unlovely, surrounded by scrubby growth and stubby hills, cluttered with houses of either pretentious rusticity or pretentious modernity. The only thing in common was water, and in Texas there was often not enough of that. Alice gave up, relaxed in the sun, reveled in technicolored memories of Henry the Eighth sweeping up the river, and, for once, did not accuse herself of being a tourist.

"You've forgotten me, haven't you?"

Startled out of her fantasies, she agreed to go below for a drink with Jerry. She hadn't forgotten him at all. His invitation, she'd thought, was only part of the chaff with Ned, not to be taken seriously. To her he was something of an apparition, too handsome to be believed, and far too young to be interested in her.

There was no one below but the barmaid, a girl about twenty, already tough looking with bleached blonde hair, a wisp of a mouth set in an ironic curve, and heavy hips cased in blue jeans. She waited on them, then began mopping the floor as if it were an ancient enemy she could never stab to death.

"Are you in school?"

"Me?" He let her know her question was incredibly naïve. "Not me. I quit to go to work when I was fifteen. My family's worked on the river for four hundred years."

She was not certain what her family had done for four hundred years. Some could be traced through a variety of occupations for about two hundred. Before that even their names were obscured in a haze of emigration.

"Where do they live?"

"Up here. Up the river across from Hampton Court. Isn't that where you're going?"

"Yes." Alice drank her bitter and kept her eyes on the barmaid, who was slamming chairs upside down on tabletops.

Abruptly, Alice asked, "How old are you?"

"Twenty-eight."

She shook her head.

"How old do you think I am?" He slid closer.

"Twenty-two?"

"Twenty-four."

"How old do you think I am?" Alice smiled wryly. Her age would surely put him off.

A boy clattered down the stairs and sat next to Jerry. Approximately the same age, but not as filled out, the look on his face was knowing, as if he'd come upon an old friend up to old tricks.

"Here's Trimmer. Have a drink with us."

"No. I've had enough already."

He seemed to be saying, "Haven't you?" But Alice sat fascinated.

"This is Alice. I'm guessing her age. How old do you think she is?"

"Thirty." Trimmer's eyes were full of laughter.

"I'm years older."

"Looks like a girl. Has a figure like one, doesn't she. Look at her!" Jerry raised his stein toward her.

Alice had a momentary look at herself standing naked on the table revolving slowly before them wrapped in a knitted dress she'd just discovered was provocative.

"Thirty-six." Jerry's voice was quickly sober.

Alice nodded. Nailed to the table, intimidated by his perception, she couldn't have moved if she'd wanted to.

"Go out with me tonight. I'll take you round to my places in East London. Show them to you."

"I . . . I can't." She despised herself for stuttering.

The barmaid hoisted chairs back down to the floor as if she were wrestling with recalcitrant bodies.

"Why not?"

"I'm married."

Jerry laughed with fine free carelessness. "What does that matter! He's not here, is he?"

"No. He's not."

"Where is he?" Trimmer had enough sense to ask.

"Back home. In America with the children."

"That's what he tells you."

"He tells me nothing." We tell each other nothing. There's never been a reason to lie. Has there? What is he doing? Alice was caught up in a tissue of questions she hadn't thought to ask herself for years. Her husband stayed at home because he had to work . . . wanted to . . . preferred to. She amended the idea as she considered it. What had been acceptable became inexplicable.

"I believe . . . Perhaps I choose to believe him."

Both boys looked at her, then Jerry said, "Come out with me tonight. There's no harm in it."

Trimmer stared at them, and Alice, aware of his eyes on her hands, wondered what he saw there.

"Are you rich?"

"Rich?" She looked up quickly, then back down at her rings. On her left hand she wore two large diamonds, on her right, an emerald surrounded by diamonds. "No. I inherited some of these. You don't have to be rich to come to Europe anymore."

Jerry picked up her left hand and twisted round the diamond that had been her grandmother's. "You look rich. You know what we'd do if we found you on the bottom of the Thames?"

Trimmer answered for him. "We'd cut that hand off."

"Really!" Alice pulled her hand out of Jerry's.

They both assured her they would. Ahh . . . they were only playing tough, trying to scare her, weren't they? She couldn't be sure. If that was the game though, she refused to be frightened.

"You're coming out with me tonight," Jerry insisted. "If you don't, I won't be able to hold my head up in front of my mates."

"Tell them I said you were too much of a man for me to handle." Alice listened to herself with faint belief in tactics of obvious flattery.

He turned to Trimmer. "What does she mean?"

"You've scared her," Trimmer said as if he didn't believe her either.

The boat stopped at a landing and Trimmer went upstairs. Against the wall on a bench the barmaid was stretched out staring at the ceiling.

"There are other girls on board," Alice offered.

"I know. I've got my eye on one." He nodded toward the upper deck.

"Ask her then."

"It's you I want."

Alice stood up. She didn't know what to do with him. She hardly knew what to do with herself. "I'm going up."

"When we get to Hampton Court, wait for me."

"I can't. Thanks for the drink." She climbed up the stairs, drifted back to an empty seat in front of the Italian lady and gazed out at Henry the Eighth's deep park beside the river. How incredible! To be thirty-six and sixteen at the same time, and to have learned nothing in between! To be chased, run, and hope to be chased again. It was all the same, just as it had been twenty years ago. Why was it impossible for her to invent a variation? No matter how she thought about her situation, nor which way she reasoned, she returned to the certainty she was unreasonably attracted to the boy. She sat down on the bench, her body bent forward, her arms wrapped around her waist as if to hold herself back.

It was all an accident, her being on the boat, talking to Ned, being available to Jerry. She was only passing through. He was only a boy who worked on the river. East London . . . Petticoat Lane . . . Billingsgate Market . . . the Tower. That's all she knew of it. Was it mostly a working-class district? What was that part of the city really like? A night going round to pubs with Jerry? Leave the rings at the hotel . . . shouldn't look like she was slumming . . . or married. The Italian lady patted her on the back, asked if she had a stomachache and Alice, tormented by the absurdity of desire, said yes, she did.

When the barge arrived at Hampton Court landing she tried to lose herself in the mass of people surging off. There was only one way to walk through, and Jerry was standing on the shore.

"Wait for me."

Alice shook her head and went past him.

He shouted something at Trimmer and followed her. "Walk with me? Just walk?"

Alice looked around. Sun shone hard on everything. The path was broad and open. There were few trees to hide behind and no tall grass to sink into. "All right."

He tried to take her arm, but she pulled away. Walking beside him she realized he was heavy, not fat, but solid. His intent was as strong as his body. They went down the path away from the barge.

"Why won't you go out with me?"

"I've told you. I'm married."

"That's nothing to do with it. Sit down."

Alice noticed many couples sitting on the grass.

"It's full daylight. I'm not going to do anything. Sit down and talk a minute." He pulled gently at her arm.

She folded her legs under her, felt grass pricking her stockings, and was ready to cry at the weakness of her flesh and her wavering will. Never, never should she have agreed to take two steps in any direction with him for he took that agreement for consent.

Sprawled on the grass beside her, he pulled at her arm once more. "Lie down."

"I will not." She sat up stiffly.

"You don't want to get to know me then?"

In this she heard an often-used complaint and could almost laugh. "Not in the way you want me to. Try to understand. There's nothing in it for you." Each word was given full weight, pronounced slowly and distinctly. As she said them she knew she lacked all goodness. An interior prompter, not a voice, but a barely sensed emanation, demanded protection. Her survival, not her marriage, was in question. She was not afraid of what he might do with her, of his taking her life or stealing her rings, but she feared self-forgetfulness.

"All right. No hard feelings." He helped her up and showed her the quickest way into Hampton Court's grounds.

She spent the afternoon wandering about palatial rooms. Their walls were covered with pictures and tapestries, and in the middle of nearly every third room was an enormous empty bed. Turning away from these she looked out of tall windows over prospects of fountains and formal gardens to shimmering reaches of water. Outside she passed through a garden thick with roses blooming so fully they were an embarrassment. Flaunting color, beauty, brevity, they waited for the nearest wind to shatter them. "Oh, how could you?" she murmured to the roses and to herself.

She was busy taking the usual picture of the lion and unicorn on top of the entrance posts when she saw the Italian lady. A few moments later, when they were crossing the bridge on their way to the train station together, Alice looked down at the barge waiting at the landing. Of course she could not see Jerry. At that distance it was impossible to discern anyone.

The Apex Man

They were a strange couple, even from a distance. She watched them coming toward her. The man was as thin as a stick. His skinny legs outlined by tight-fitting blue jeans had a convalescent appearance, and when the wind blew his shirt against his chest she saw that despite the fact that his shirt hung from relatively broad shoulders, the rest of his body was as emaciated as his legs. His head dominated. Long and broad at the same time, it was almost too big for the neck that supported it. The brow and jaw were both wide, and the chin so long it seemed as pointed as one of Picasso's triangular portraits. He had one arm around the shoulders of a girl who was his opposite in every way except height. They were both short people, but she was all bumps and curves and roundness, a bulging sausage of a girl stuffed into green pants and a sweater. Her dark hair was gathered into a fat bunch on top of her head while his, fair and straight, blew lankly around his ears. They talked and nodded, staring ahead into some sort of special lovers' unreality. Mrs. Drake watched them cross the street, and was so transfixed by their strangeness she didn't take advantage of the gap in traffic to maneuver her car across. She felt she must wait to see them safely on the other side for they seemed absolutely unaware of cars, the girl simply rolling along, a movable prop for the young man. Without her how could he make his way through the world? Maybe he had a job he was peculiarly fit to do. He could be a circus performer, an acrobat. Or perhaps he was the top man in one of those balancing acts, the apex of a pyramid of strong men holding others on their shoulders, and this smallest one was the last one, the one who stood on top.

When they were safely across the street Mrs. Drake drove on to the grocery store, where she chose strawberry ice cream, green vegetables, potatoes, a loaf of bread, a rump roast, some canned beans which were marked down three cents, and, in a rare moment of whimsy, plucked a can of tomato juice from the top of a pyramid.

When she got home with four sacks of groceries, a whole week's supply of food, she rested in the car a moment. Doing a week's grocery shopping was tiresome. She got tired of wheeling the basket up and down aisles, trying all the time to make decisions about what to have for supper, wondering what Richard would like . . . strange to be wondering again what a man would like for supper. It was eleven years, twelve in July, since she'd seen the last of Mr. Drake. Those first few years after his death she'd been a widow grieving and remembering. Time had taken care of that first harsh grief and her memories of her husband were—until Richard came home—usually of the beginning, happier years of their marriage. He'd died of injuries after a car wreck, an accident of his own making—driving while intoxicated, the policeman said. He didn't know Mr. Drake had been walking, running, sleeping, working while intoxicated for at least ten years. Thank God no one else was killed! He crashed into an empty parked car. When he was gone, Mrs. Drake drove more carefully than ever, reproached herself occasionally for the vague feeling of relief she felt, and slipped gradually from widowhood to spinsterhood. The insurance money was carefully invested and she turned the upper story of their home into an apartment. She lived in the apartment below, alone but comforted by the sounds of footsteps upstairs. They protected her from what she called, with an appropriate sniff, "old ladies' fears," terrors of noises in the night and strange knocks at the door. She knew those terrors. Mr. Drake had left her in the house by herself late many a night. She'd sit up in bed quivering, listening to something that could be a tree limb brushing a screen—or someone stealthily creeping through the back door. And the strange knock? It was generally one of her husband's friends delivering him, bringing him home like a postman delivering a badly wrapped parcel, one with loose string and ripped paper. Mr. Drake's tie was always untied and his coat off or lost. But it could be the leering face she'd seen once, nose pressed against the upper glass panes of the door, mouth gaping in a demonic grin. She screamed. He ran. After seeing the face she slept with a meat hammer under her pillow and a broom propped against the side of the bed. "Watcha going to do, sweep the devil away?" Mr. Drake used to ask. "It's a good weapon for a woman," Mrs. Drake replied staunchly, and kept it there. One morning she'd come in and found him brandishing it at one of his imaginary devils he said was standing in the corner.

When her husband died and the first tenants moved in she arranged a signal. The broom bumping against the ceiling, the floor of the upstairs bedroom, meant "Help!" Fortified in this way, she relaxed. Then her son, Richard, started getting divorced and came home—to stay it seemed.

Mrs. Drake sat in the car and wondered if she honked would Richard come down and carry the groceries in for her? He needed privacy, he said, so she'd let him have the upstairs apartment when the last renters were gone. She knew, after living with Mr. Drake, about the need for privacy. Richard saw her only at mealtimes. She hated to honk, to sit out at the curb making a lot of noise, demanding service. What if she did let him have the apartment rent free? What if she did support him for a while? He didn't have a summer job. He was her only child. He needed it, and she wasn't going to demand he repay her by running errands. She poked the strawberry ice cream carton cautiously with one finger. Getting soft. Might as well start taking things in. Richard might hear her and offer to come down and help. Mrs. Drake got out of her car with one sack and slammed the door. Her son didn't appear, however, until she was on the way in with the fourth sack. He looked sleepy. She'd heard him get in his car and drive off sometime in the night. Determined not to stay awake worrying, she made herself go back to sleep, but she woke up again when he came home around three, a familiar hour, Mr. Drake's favorite time for rolling home. "Rolling home, rolling home, by the light of the sil-ver-ry moo-oo-oon," he'd sing, when he was able to sing. She'd get up to let him in. For years after he was gone she'd find herself wide awake at 3:00 A.M. waiting for someone.

"Here, Mother, let me carry that for you."

He took the heavy sack from her with easy male insistence on doing a favor for a woman. She'd missed that. She used to think she wouldn't care if Mr. Drake came home drunk every night of the world as long as he didn't grumble about carrying things in and taking the garbage out.

"Where do you want this?"

"Over there." She pointed to the kitchen table already loaded with sacks. Richard shoved them all over to one corner and sat down.

"Mother, could I have some coffee and orange juice?"

"Yes, of course. Just a minute." She paused to gaze at the sacks. Which one was hiding the frozen orange juice?

"What are you digging around for?"

"The juice."

"I don't have to have orange juice."

"There isn't any other kind. I don't have anything else here— Oh!"

"What?"

"Here's some tomato juice. I forgot I bought it." She pulled the can out and began shaking it vigorously.

"Do you do that often, forget what you buy at the store?"

"All the time. It's the only fun of going shopping, the surprises you find when you get home."

"Impulse buying," Richard said. "You must buy a lot of things you don't need that way." He poured himself some coffee. "Your father used to say the same thing." It slipped out before she thought, but it was so like Mr. Drake. He teased her about impulse buying every time she came home from the store.

"Did he? I didn't know he ever noticed things like groceries."

"He was a sharp man. How else could he have carried on his law practice?" Why couldn't she stop? She knew Richard didn't like for her to talk about his father. Somehow he always pressed her to it, though. They'd be talking about the simplest everyday things and there'd be Mr. Drake, drifting in like a ghost, demanding she defend him to his son.

"You miss him, don't you? You even miss all the noise, the singing and shouting and pounding!"

"It's been a lot quieter around here these last twelve years," she said amiably. "Here's your juice."

He started to take the glass from her, then flattened his palm against it. Juice sloshed out of the glass all over her hand.

"What's the matter? I thought you liked tomato."

"I do, but it's too acid."

"Richard, orange juice is acid, too." She put the glass down and wiped her hand with a wet dishrag.

"I know. I forgot."

"If you've really got ulcers you shouldn't be drinking coffee either. At least I don't think it's supposed to be good for ulcers."

"You don't believe it's ulcers?" He blinked his eyes slowly at her.

"It's not like not believing in God, Richard."

"What in the name of heaven does God have to do with my ulcers?"

She giggled helplessly while he stared at her. "Nothing. I'm sorry. You ought to see a doctor."

"I saw one in Houston. He said it sounded like ulcers."

"Yes, I remember. You told me before. That doctor sounds like a quack to me. Did he give you any tests?"

"No."

"Did he say anything about tests?"

"He told me to come back for them, but—"

"But you didn't!"

He drew circles with one finger in a blob of spilled coffee. "I hate to take the damn tests. He was going to make me drink a lot of stuff and X-ray me."

"It's the only way they can find out about ulcers. Let me make an appointment for you with Dr. Schwartz."

"Oh, Mother!" he sighed.

"You need to find out about things like that. I'm going to call Schwartz today."

He drew some more circles in the spilled coffee.

"Richard, don't you want to know if you've actually got ulcers?"

"I'm—I don't want to be operated on."

"Who said anything about operating? You always think the worst possible things are going to happen. They cure ulcers all the time by giving people medicine and keeping them on bland diets. If you're afraid of surgery the best thing to do is see a doctor now before you have to have surgery. Sitting around worrying about it will only make—"

"All right!"

"Well sometimes I think you enjoy agonizing over things."

"You sound like Laura."

It wasn't the first time he'd mentioned his wife's name. When he first came home he'd said he didn't want to talk about the divorce so she hadn't asked him about it. She'd kept absolutely silent on the subject, but Richard was always on the verge of telling her everything.

"You didn't sleep well last night, did you?"

"Oh, did I wake you up?"

He answered her with such an air of fake innocence she wanted to shake him, to grab both his shoulders and shake him good. He wanted attention so badly.

"No, you didn't wake me. I thought you looked tired."

"I don't sleep well any night. I did at first when I came home, but I don't anymore. I try to read. Then I get in the car and drive around."

"Where?"

"Just around."

Dangerous, dangerous as could be, and that was what she wanted to tell him, that driving aimlessly around until three in the morning was dangerous. Look where driving around got your father! No, she wasn't going to tell him that. She was supposed to exclaim, to cry out, Don't, my son! You must take care of yourself. Let Mother take care of you, poor child, poor little boy. What a mean, nasty bitch your wife is to leave you alone, sleepless at night, alone in bed. Here's a teddy bear. You can go to sleep with old bear. Think about good things. Think about merry-go-rounds, birthday parties, ponies, puppy dogs. She could feel the small boy's head under her hand, the soft hair smoothed by her palm. She looked over at Richard's bald spot and wondered if she had made it. Had she worn away the hair rubbing his head? Poor Richard. He had finished his coffee and was absently stroking the top of his head, trying to cover the bald spot with a few thin hairs.

He'd gone without a haircut for some time now. He ought not to let himself go like that. Another week or so and his hair would be as long as the strange man's she'd seen early that morning. She thought of telling him about the little man who drifted along held up by the stout girl. She wanted to ask him if there was such a thing as an apex man in a circus balancing act. Again, she checked herself. Richard would not be interested in her speculations about peculiar-looking people. He could only be interested in questions about his own problems.

"Richard, if you get a divorce, when will it be final?"

"I'm not getting a divorce. It's Laura who says she wants one."

"Do you think she'll go through with it?"

"I don't know. How am I to know?"

"Haven't you talked to her?"

"Yes."

"Well?"

"I still don't know." Pushing his chair back, he got up and started out the door. She would have liked to ask him where he was going, but she was not going to ask him one more question that morning.

Mrs. Drake found a clean cup, poured herself some coffee, and sat down at the table surrounded by tin cans, vegetables, and the ice cream beginning to melt and run in pink streaks down the sides of the carton. Rising quickly, she grabbed it and stuck it in the freezer. Then she sat down again. The chiming clock in the living room rang eleven—morning almost gone. There were still groceries to put away and she should go upstairs to make Richard's bed at least. He'd told her not to bother. Sometimes she didn't. The stairs were steep, too steep for a woman sixty-two years old to be climbing every day. When she did go up she was appalled by Richard's filth. How could one rather small man make such a mess? She'd tried to teach him as a child to be neat, not fussy, but neat. Someday he'd have a wife who would appreciate neatness. That lesson, like some others, hadn't taken. He left dirty shirts on the floor, threw his pants over the backs of chairs without bothering to see if the creases were straight, dripped ashes all around an overflowing ashtray, let his ties slide off the rack in the closet, pulled the shades down crooked, and tied the curtains back in big knots when they got in the way. Tiresome . . . made her peevish to think about what she'd surely find up there. There was nothing in the least odd about Richard's messes. She wouldn't have minded finding all his dirty clothes under the bed, a collection of silk top hats on the dresser, or funny faces drawn on the windows. Mr. Drake had done that once after she'd seen the face at the door. All she'd find in Richard's room, though, was the listless sort of dirt made by a man who refused to take care of himself.

She hadn't seen any liquor up there yet and wouldn't open the bureau drawers, not because it was an invasion of privacy; she was afraid of seeing a whisky bottle rolling toward her out from under a heap of clean socks, afraid of seeing the vicious brown liquid rocking back and forth in its bottle.

She was certain he drank. When he was in high school he'd come home one night, or rather was delivered like his father by two staggering friends. The next day he sat around shamefaced and quiet until she told him, "It's all right. You've got to experiment sometime. I don't expect you not to drink. You don't have to take a pledge." Moderation was all she required. She knew she'd have to be moderate as well. She wouldn't gain a thing by pleading, crying, or losing her temper, much as she wanted to do all three.

"I should know better." He gave her a weak grin. "I don't want to turn out like Dad. You don't need another alcoholic in the family, do you, Mother?"

"No."

"You think I'm going to be like him, don't you? I mean . . . maybe it's inherited?"

"You are not going to be like your father."

"Why not?"

I won't let you. That's why. I won't allow it to happen. She stood glaring at him in determined silence, then said, "It's not inherited. That's only an excuse."

"Mother, have you ever taken a drink?"

"Yes."

"But you don't drink at all now. Did you ever, in college maybe?"

"No. I don't like the taste of it."

"I do," said Richard and ducked his head.

She left him studying his hands. If she hadn't walked out she would have screamed at him—not words. She had no words in her mind, only an unintelligible scream.

He probably drank too much at other times. She didn't know about them, didn't want to know. Mrs. Drake heaved herself up out of the chair, flicked her fingers over the tin cans like a pianist trying to decide which chord to hit, picked up two cans, and started to the pantry. When Richard was a little boy he'd played grocery store out there, shifting the cans on the shelves, selling them to imaginary people and to her while she cooked supper, a meal they ate alone together. Mr. Drake seldom got home for supper as it was his custom to go to the bar immediately after work. She and Richard ate together every night. He'd tell her what happened at nursery school, at grammar school, at high school; she'd correct his table manners and tell him the details of her day. She had to be careful not to let him become a mama's boy. She pushed him out to play with other children. He always came home. Then she'd get angry and tell him he had to stay outside.

"Go play. Play with the other children."

"I don't want to."

"Go anyway."

He'd go off for a little while, but he'd come back. "Mama, I hurt my knee." "I fell down." "Mama, I cut my finger."

It was only a stage, she consoled herself, only a stage all children went through. He loved Band-Aids. Didn't all kids? For a few weeks she refused to buy any more. Richard kept falling down.

"Scabbiest kid I ever saw," said Mr. Drake.

"He wouldn't be if you paid him some attention."

"What do you mean? I'm paying attention. I see him."

"The only thing you—" She was going to say the only thing he paid any real attention to was the level of bourbon left in a bottle, but, knowing the rage she could evoke, she cut herself off with a loud "Humph!" She'd had plenty of all that—the shouting, the rage, and she wasn't going to do it any more. There was just so much of her, not enough to divide between fighting with her husband and being a mother to Richard at the same time. Richard needed so much. Not material things, those were managed; he needed affection. Richard was a glutton for love. She gave him all she had, holding back nothing though she was fearful all the time she'd smother him with it. She was more grateful than he for every friend he had. Then there were girls. They seemed to like him. She kept up with them all. Finally, when he went to college—he'd gone to SMU right there in Dallas instead of going away to school—there was Laura.

She was exactly the sort of girl Richard needed, stable, thoughtful, pretty though a bit plump. Mrs. Drake was a bit plump herself so she didn't hold that against anybody. After he married Laura, Richard, who'd always been small and thin, began taking on some weight. They had an apartment in town until they finished graduate school. Mrs. Drake didn't see them often, once every two weeks for Sunday dinner at their place or hers. For once in her life she luxuriated in the clichés of happiness: Richard and Laura were a perfect match, a mathematician married to a musician. Richard was untidy; Laura was a good housekeeper. He was a glutton for love; she was overflowing with affection. He had his special chair, his special dishes, his important research. Laura made him comfortable, fed him, and played the piano beautifully. If she was relegated to making background music, it was good music. She had her practice hours to herself and someday she would have her own pupils. Balance, Mrs. Drake thought, balance was everything. She gave herself up to giddy dreams of a perfect pair of grandchildren, but there were none. Children would come later, they assured her. Right then they had to get through school and find jobs. They'd done all that, including finding jobs in Houston, and now, after four years of apparently happy marriage, Laura wanted a divorce.

Mrs. Drake banged the door of a cupboard shut. She was through putting up the wretched groceries. While she was considering taking herself out to lunch as a kind of reward, the phone rang.

"Mrs. Drake, is Richard there?"

"No. Laura, it's so good to hear your voice. He's gone out somewhere. Could I have him call you?"

"No! I don't want to talk to him. He calls me all the time from up there, but he uses a pay phone at some bar. I only wanted to make sure he was staying with you. I thought he was."

"He calls you from a bar? Why? He could use the phone here any time."

"Well, I guess— You know he drinks?"

"Yes, but I didn't know— How much does he drink?"

"Quite a bit. Sometimes I think he's trying to beat his father's record. Oh, how awful of me! I shouldn't have—"

"That's all right. We all know about Mr. Drake. Where are you calling from?"

"I'm in Houston."

"The connection is so clear, I couldn't tell. I was hoping you were in town. I'd like to see you. I'm so sorry about you and Richard. I thought perhaps this was just a separation."

"Did Richard tell you that?"

"No, not exactly." She paused and pulled at the kinked phone cord. It curled back up the minute she let it go. "He says he doesn't want to talk about it, but I think he really does. He acts like he doesn't know what's going to happen next."

"He ought to know by now. I've told him. He doesn't want anything to happen. He wants to let things drift on and on. He agreed not to contest the divorce, but he left without signing anything. A process server is supposed to bring him the papers today, this afternoon in fact. It's just a formality, but I wanted to be sure he was staying with you. The man's got to hand him the papers. I told him to check there first, then I thought I'd make sure." Her voice dwindled away.

In a desperate attempt to hold on to Laura, Mrs. Drake asked, "Did Richard ever say anything to you about his ulcers?"

"Yes, but he won't do anything about them. I made him go to the doctor once. I even went with him, but he wouldn't go back for the tests. You know how he is. And, whatever he's got, drinking won't help. I know I shouldn't be saying this to you, but I thought you'd understand. I can't change him, and I've helped him all I can. Mrs. Drake, didn't you ever think about divorcing your husband?"

"Of course I thought about it, but there was Richard. We were different somehow."

"The difference is you're stronger than I am."

"Perhaps I'm weaker."

"I don't think so. You've never seemed that way to me."

There was so much kindness in Laura's young voice Mrs. Drake felt she was going to start crying. She pulled herself up straight against the wall. "I'm sorry, Laura."

"So am I. I loved Richard, but I can't back him up any longer, and I can't live with him the way he is."

They said goodbye. Mrs. Drake put the receiver back on the hook and sagged down in the nearest chair. An alcoholic father, an alcoholic son. Classic. But, no, they were different. Mr. Drake was a robust drunkard. He howled and roared against a terrible world. "The depravity of man!" he'd shout in his blackest moments. "Cursed are the stars that led me to this course!" She didn't know where he'd gotten the line, but he'd made it his own. Being a criminal lawyer didn't help his outlook any. No matter how he struggled he was caught in paradox. "Law and order. We must have law and order!" Every table in the house suffered from his pounding, and sometimes he'd emphasize the words by pounding his knee. Then he'd be in court the following day defending some poor wretch against the strictness of law and order. That was his reverse side, his belief in the rights of everybody. He used to tell her about some of his clients. "If only he'd finished high school . . . if only she hadn't gotten pregnant . . . if only . . ." He found excuses for them all, but as the years wore on he ran out of excuses or quit believing in them. He could not, however, wear out his compassion, though he tried to protect himself with cynicism. "Some people are just sorry," he'd say. In his sorrow for them, he drank. At times he was happily drunk. Those were the nights he came home singing, "By the light of the sil-ver-ry moo-oo-oon," and she would get out of bed to lead him in. There were probably other deeper reasons for his drinking, but she'd reached the limit of her understanding about Mr. Drake. She couldn't go on asking why, why, why forever. Some people were just sorry and some men just drank.

But Richard— Richard was not his father all over again. The one time she'd seen him drunk he was neither raging nor singing. He was quiet and ashamed . . . only a boy then. Now he was almost thirty years old and all she knew was he went to bars and called his wife because she was divorcing him. He had a good wife and a profession he seemed to like. What could be more orderly than the study of mathematics? What could be more removed from the daily paradoxes his father had tried to escape? Richard had a well-ordered existence. He taught his classes, went to his office, talked to students, graded papers, and did research on something or other. She imagined him standing in front of a board filled with geometric figures. He was neatly dressed in the sport coat and slacks she'd given him last Christmas. With a piece of chalk in one hand he was carefully re-tracing the outline of a triangle, chanting professorially a theorem ending in a logical conclusion. He was not standing before a judge pleading for the rights of some no-count who'd stabbed another fool in a knife fight. And he had an audience, too, plenty of attention, thirty-some-odd students in three different classes, ninety or more people hanging on to his every word. What was Richard trying to escape?

Did Laura seriously mean he was trying to beat his father's record? As if there were a record, as if anybody had ever marked an X on the barroom wall for every bottle of beer or bourbon Mr. Drake had consumed! She laughed at a momentary vision of X's winding around the room. Mr. Drake might have done it himself. He had the ability to make fun of his own weakness. Richard didn't.

If he was trying to compete with his father's drinking— Mrs. Drake shuddered. The idea raised gooseflesh on her bare arms. "Mr. Drake," she said aloud, and shuddered again. She'd talked to him a lot out loud at first. Then she'd let grief die and cured herself of her ghostly conversations. Here she was at it again after almost twelve years' silence. Richard's coming did bring his father back so. "Mr. Drake," she said petulantly, "your son's on the booze."

She was sitting in the front room looking at the newspaper when the process server came. He was such an ordinary-looking man she thought at first he was an insurance salesman.

"Does Richard Drake live here?"

"Not here, upstairs." She crumpled the paper in her lap and sat still listening to Richard's bell ring, his steps coming downstairs, him and the man going upstairs together. She could hear the murmur of their voices, but not what they were saying. The process server came downstairs by himself. In a few minutes she heard Richard's footsteps descending slowly. His door slammed. Still clutching the paper, she went to the window and saw him drive away.

Should have told him what was coming, she thought. But what difference would it have made? He didn't want to know. He'd rather remain in limbo the rest of his life.

It was late when he returned and there were some other people with him. She heard them running upstairs singing loudly as they went. She didn't know the tune, but identified it as one of those cowboy songs about rambling and gambling and hopeless love—a strange song for a mathematics professor to be singing.

Mrs. Drake dozed off again to waken to the sound of something heavy falling down the stairs, voices shouting, car lights coming in her window. She jumped out of bed, put on a robe, and went to Richard's door. It was wide open and behind it was Richard sitting on the last step with his head on his knees. There was a trail of blood on the carpet of the stairs. A man's voice behind her said, "We got to take him to the hospital."

She smelled whiskey in the air all around her. "What happened?"

"We were trying to put him to bed. He wanted to go out again."

Richard raised his head. Blood trickled down his face.

Another voice said, "It's the top of his head that's cut. We got to get him to the hospital . . . 'mergency ward there."

She turned to see him leaning against the post by the steps. "You'd better watch out or you'll fall!" she shrieked.

"I fell, Mama," Richard wailed. "I fell down the stairs and hurt my head."

She bent down to him and put one hand on his shoulder. "I know, son. We're going to take you to the hospital and get it bandaged. Here!" She straightened up and called to the two strange men, "Help me carry him."

The Accidental Trip to Jamaica

It was an accident, our going to Jamaica, and you had to prove you'd been there by crawling around on the bottom of the too-blue sea to snitch a piece of coral I carried home. When I got back my students asked me, "Where have you been?" They demanded to know because I'm not Mrs. Somebody-or-Other but somebody they know. That's the way they are these days, knowing. I did not tell them. Not many school teachers go to Jamaica in January or any other month, and they would not have understood. I put the coral next to a papier-mâché dinosaur made by my middle child. It's a striped blue and green dinosaur as blue and green as the water at Ocho Rios. I thought it fit, made a pair of things. The shape of the dinosaur and the coral finger are the same. They are both disasters, one belonging to a prehistoric past, one belonging to a month ago. Yet the dinosaur still inhabits the earth—SEE GIANT DINOSAUR TRACKS FIVE MILES OFF THIS HIGHWAY—and the coral is the unmoving finger which wrote FOLLY.

Why did we go? Why didn't we stay here? The weather was just as peculiar at home. It snowed twice that week for the first time in seven years. I wonder and you float. You always float, not in my dreams, in my wakefulness.

AUSTIN DENTIST DROWNS IN JAMAICA

Is it real? Yes, as real as birds in trees or gritty bits of sand in shoes.

There's blood in the sad-dul.
There's blood on the ground.
And a great big pud-dul of blood all around.

Cowboys don't go to Jamaica. They go home on the range. But we went, you in your white linen cowboy suit and me looking like a well-kept go-go girl though the go-go girls have all gone. A woman has to have some sense of history to be a well-kept anachronism. You always wanted to be a cowboy and I always wanted to be anything but a school teacher. We met dressed in our disguises, our everyday clothes worn over our everyday lives.

Two secrets are clawing each other inside my head: 1) you are dead; 2) we went to Jamaica together. I have told the most cunning lies. Mother lives in Florida, which accounts for my tan. She believes I was in New York seeing plays every noon and being pursued by murderous addicts every night. My husband believes I went to New York, then to Florida. They do not talk to each other often, but if they ever do Mother is so forgetful now that I can convince her I was in Florida in January and she forgot.

Why did we go to Jamaica?

We were going to Sun Valley. Skiing. At least you were.

We had to buy all new tropical clothes. Mine are still hidden in a locker at the Dallas airport. The Goodwill Store or the Sisters of Charity or whoever gets clothes left in airport lockers is going to get a mess of batik, two bikinis, and lots of black nylon panties and bras, your fetish, not mine.

You are floating on a whim.

That's what took us there. My whim. I had never been to Jamaica. I had never been to Sun Valley either. You said why not and I said I don't go places like that. You said I was an over-sheltered academic intellectual. We nearly parted then. I said don't speak to me of shelter. I worked my way through undergraduate school as a waitress.

There is an ancient rule written in the back of every woman's head: Don't go anywhere with a strange man.

I erased the rule.

You had some rules of your own. You tucked them in and pulled the covers over their heads.

Whim ruled.

The first whim you had was the white cowboy suit. We laughed all the way to Neiman-Marcus in the taxi and all the way back. Then we got on lots of planes and flew to Jamaica. The last one had a black stewardess with a British accent. She was so exactly right we made her talk as much as we could. She told us about Blue Mountain Coffee, Appleton Rum, the tiny beaches of Ocho Rios and Dunns River Falls.

Please quit floating!

She was a treasure, that girl. She also told us about the kinky Englishman's restaurant on the way to Ocho Rios. You re-mem-bah him, don't you, the one who tied the cardboard flowers on his almond tree to fool the *National Geographic* photographer. His name was Clive, or Cliff, or Clown. The centers of his flowers were inverted pop-bottle tops sprayed orange. The *National Geographic* man was not fooled; we were, I would have liked a picture of the almond tree in bloom, but we'd sworn off cameras.

At Ocho Rios I wanted to stay in one of those immense, immaculate, secluded hotels, and you insisted I had to see how the other half lives so we had to go to the one with bunny rabbits on the carpet. Miles and miles of ears—someone's idea of how the middle class would like to sin, walking on rabbits' heads. The bathtub was black, seven feet long, three feet deep. It was big enough for copulation, large enough for sleeping, deep enough for drowning if you were drunk and you were not. That bathtub was meet, and fit, and right for the scene, a lovely prop. The couch was all right too, even to its pretend leather cover, but the beds were twins. Very strange. I should have packed up and gone to Florida the minute I laid eyes on those beds.

You said, "That is not how a kept woman behaves."

I said, "Dear Amy Vanderbilt, What are the rules of behavior for a kept woman?"

We couldn't put them together. A light fixture and a table were rooted to the wall between. Do you think the owner of the bunny rabbits believes his guests would cram lights and side tables into their suitcases along with his hotel towels?

"Ring for room service! Call out the housekeeper!"

No. We had a do-it-yourself fit. It wasn't hard to lift the mattresses off the beds and put them side by side on the floor. I had a practical housewife's fit. "How can anybody make up beds like that?" You assured me, "Nobody is going to make up this bed." I thought, "How squalid!" but I kept that to myself. Discretion is the better part of vice. New rules have to be made all the time. I may write that to Ms. V.

I flang myself into the bathtub. You flang yourself right after me. Relaxation was what I craved. You craved fornication, difficult in the bathtub. Too slippery. In bed we fell. You drilled me, your dentistical metaphor, not mine. We are all hung up by the tools of our trade.

"Rum and Coca-Cola."

"That's a song my mother used to sing. Now I drink it every afternoon when I come in from school and the oldest child is playing the piano. Yesterday my husband discovered me sitting on the piano bench with drink in hand trying to pick out the tune with one finger. Elusive, that tune. What is the second line? Tomorrow I will give my students ten extra points on a ten-minute quiz if they can tell me the second line. They won't be able to.

Where was I?

What will the Little Flowers of Mercy or the Brothers of St. Poverty do with your skis you left in the men's room of the old Dallas airport at Love Field?

Did love have anything to do with it? I think not. We were two people who had arrived at middle age, that time in life, like adolescence, when we were convinced nothing else was ever going to happen to us. We had to grab fate by the shirt collar. We had to make something happen.

Could you quit floating?

You loved the girls in bikinis with bunny-rabbit tails. It followed that I had to buy the bikini but go tailless into the Caribbean. While you went to ask the manager for a tail for your wife, I went swimming.

Rabbits have no tails atall, tails atall,
Rabbits have no tails atall,
Just a pow-der puff.

Same song, second verse.
Could be better,
But it's gonna be worse.

Rabbits have no tails atall . . .

That's a song my youngest brought home from camp. The youngest sings, the middle one makes papier-mâché dinosaurs, the oldest one plays rock piano. My husband does gravestone rubbings. I have already ordered mine so he can rub while waiting. My epitaph is: Here Lies Melissa Hawkins. She Finally Left Texas. Doing myself in? No, not I. Ennui causes tombstones to be ordered ahead of time. To live in Texas is to live in ennui. I've never liked the landscape here, a great blah, half of it creeping toward the desert to be dried out, half of it oozing toward the Gulf to dirty up the continental shelf. Jamaica was most beautiful, a garden rioting above the sea.

I was in the water floating when you arrived with the bad news.

"The Bunny Mother is very particular about the tails."

She would not sell one, give one, or trade one to a cowboy in tropic white. We consulted. You bought three powder puffs which I cleverly pinned together and sewed onto my black panties. Dear Heloise, I was the one who wrote you asking for directions for rabbit tail construction. Signed: Melissa Makedo. The pins clanked together. For some things there are no substitutes. We had to be content with the ghost of James Bond playing ping-pong with Malcolm X reincarnated in a dashiki. We had to put up with an alloyed steel band. But you cried out when I pinched you. It was real, as real as sun in rum and poinciana blooms in hair.

Oh, what's to do?

Everything would have been all right if you hadn't insisted on the expeditions. A small run-away vacation is simple if you keep it to bed, beach, and bar. Not for you though. You had to see things, to be instructed. We went to Kingston to find Harry Belafonte. He wasn't there. It was hot. There were no ships in the harbor. Port Royal was still mostly under water. The guide kept saying, "Whiskey!" and I kept telling him we didn't have a camera. His disappointment followed us to Bremmer Hall. Did he put a hex on us? You noticed he had beautiful teeth. Nobody else did. Bananas grow up; they point their baby fingers to the sky. That's what I learned at Bremmer Hall. The overseer waited to hear the camera click. Everything was going wrong.

"The other half lives with cameras," I said.

"Never mind," you said.

So, I neverminded awhile.

An interlude, a lull.

"We'll learn to scuba dive."

"OK." But I didn't like the look of the weights they hang around a diver's waist.

> Full fathom five thy father lies
> With lead weights about his waist.

Literature is instructive.

I took up the snorkel.

> I must down to the seas again,
> To the lonely sea and the sky.

We went down in an elevator, the only time we used it.

"Is this how the other half lives?"

You said indeed it was.

The elevator opened on the beach. We walked to the pier carrying our flippers, looking quite pro. Out into the blue we rocked in a glass-bottomed boat. You swam under the boat and broke off the piece of coral. I watched. Our instructor went in after you. Wilson was his name. You re-mem-bah Wilson, don't you? He was the one who forgot to warn you sea urchins sting. Yeah, Wilson. Skinny. Wore a red nylon bathing suit. His teeth were filed to sharp points. Wilson. Vampire Man we called him after you came up bloody with sea urchin spines. You were a trifle hysterical then, babbling about sea horses and underwater rodeos. Wilson wanted to hit you. I shook my head. Years of pedagogy were behind that head shake. He held his hand.

The interlude was over. Back to the expeditions, to the last expedition. Dunns River Falls falls hundreds of feet to the sea. The thing to do is to walk up it with a native guide—Tarzan climbing up the boulders through the spray. We approached by sea. Wilson sailed us within the reef all the way.

I said, "Must we?"

"Yes," you said.

Fatal, that yes. Are you floating on your own whim? Where does the truth lie? It lies, and lies, and lies.

On the beach below Dunns River Falls there was a gang of tourists. A black man danced in the midst of them balancing a tray full of rum drinks covered with hibiscus blossoms. Another black man wove green bamboo fronds into hats. Another black man made violins from hollow bamboo canes. He rosined the bow with sea water. Very industrious people, those Jamaicans. What is the Salvation Army going to do with a bamboo hat gone brown and a dried-up bamboo violin? My souvenirs. We danced the limbo with the tourists. Dear Arthur Murray, Do you need a limbo teacher? Inspired by mass frivolity, I played "The Blue Danube Waltz" on my new violin.

That's when we got separated.

A student is standing by my desk. He wants to know why he's failing the course.

I tell him we are all failing the course.

How did we get separated? Some spirit of misadventure lured me. Other people, friendly tourists, took my hands. We formed a human chain. The one who got to hold the guide's hand was the luckiest. I saw you far below holding hands with two strangers. I could not shout. The guides did all the shouting, ha-lo-o-ing over booming water, screeching like mad parrots. We climbed. I watched where I was going. The water was icy; slippery rocks spewed jets of spray. All around the jungle hung. At a turn you saw me and lifted your hand to wave, wrenching yourself loose from the human chain. You were miles below, but I saw you fall. Your body slithered toward the sea. Everyone in your chain stopped while the guide pulled everyone in mine on up. You floated top side down, the deadman's float. I knew it. I passed my Red Cross beginner's test. Our guide was busy imitating the mating call of mynah birds. He saw nothing but the boulders in front of him. The chain of hands pulled me over the boulders. I looked again and saw you floating. Still. People were staring at your back.

I took the coward's choice. Because your life was over, should mine be ruined? Before we had whims. Now decisions were to be made. In my bikini shielded by a see-through shirt, intensely vulnerable and thoroughly shocked, I stepped out of the jungle to the car park and hailed a cab. Back at the rabbit warren I collected my things and dressed myself with lively trembling fingers. Oh, so carefully I printed your name in large, block, childish letters on an envelope. Inside I folded one piece of paper with the following message: Go home to your wife and children. That's all you ever talk about anyway. Signed: Suzy Floozie. Your wife was going to have to pay your double-room hotel bill. It was the most I could do for her. I stomped up to the hotel clerk, simulating our first and only lover's quarrel, pretending great anger which was not hard. Anger is near to fear, neighbor to grief.

"Put this in Dr. Grodall's box." I shoved the envelope over the black marble counter. Funereal. Dear Mr. Rabbit, Down at your hotel in Jamaica sex and death clasp hands and hold on for dear life. Something needs to be done about the ambiance. Love and kisses, Slutina Mae Harlot.

I didn't say please. Tears dribbled down my cheeks. Most undignified.

Slamming out of the hotel was easy. So many doors. Bang! Bang! Bang! July 4th exit. Cab again. Airport again. Only plane there was flying to England. I flew.

"You didn't!" That's what you'd say, your right eyebrow a lofty arch. You used to practice raising your eyebrows in the bathroom mirror.

I did. I must have. There's a ten-pence piece in my coin purse. I bite it now and then to remind myself I went.

London. January. Raining. Cold. Not much money. I couldn't stay

inside the bed and breakfast all day. Wallpaper roses swagged and
bunched and swagged. Dizzifying. Dear Dorothy Draper, London
needs you. All night I circled the walls with the roses while you
floated face down.

> Roses are red.
> My toes are blue.
> I will quit floating
> If you will too.

Dear Witch of the West, Could you send me the spell for laying a
ghost? Ten pence remuneration enclosed.

I rented a raccoon fur coat (unendangered species) from a costume shop, highly reputed, costumers to H. M. the Queen. MARKS
AND SPENCER HAVE GALOSHES CHEAP. An Italian maitre d'
at a restaurant in Soho gave me an umbrella left behind by an Englishman emigrating to Australia.

I went to the National Gallery, looked at Venus, Cupid, Folly, and
Time and decided it's time I went home.

Art is instructive if you're ready to be instructed.

Three students are standing at my desk. They want to know if they
have to take the final examination. I tell them, no. They are going to
take it anyway. The course I teach is English 60002.Q. The 19th
Century Romantic Novel. The real title is The Will to Fail. Those
three will pass, which means they have learned nothing.

Planes again. Airports. Home. Austin Public Library. Newspaper
files.

AUSTIN DENTIST DROWNS IN JAMAICA

If we hadn't had two hours between planes a month ago— If you
hadn't started talking to me— If I could have gotten to New York
without going through Dallas— If we hadn't sat next to each other
on the plane from Austin to Dallas, I could still be a not-too-shel-
tered academic intellectual and you could be back in your office with
a sprained ankle complaining about the ski patrol at Sun Valley.
Maybe.

Why do you keep on floating?

If I had slipped, I would not haunt you.

Dear Carroll Righter, I was born under the sign of Aries, the Ram, at 3 A.M. on the morning of April 7th. Is tomorrow a good day for sending messages?

I'm putting this in an empty rum bottle, one I emptied while I wrote. Tomorrow the bottle will be dropped into the Colorado River, which flows to the Gulf, which mingles with many seas. The final message is: SINK, PLEASE.

My Brother Is a Cowboy

My daddy used to advise my brother and me, "Don't tell everything you know." This was his golden rule. I keep it in mind as I constantly disregard it. I've been busy most of my life telling everything I know. My brother Kenyon took it to heart. He tells nothing, not even the most ordinary answers to questions about his everyday existence. If my mother asks when he'll be home for supper, he says, "I don't know." The nearest he'll come to giving the hour for when he'll come in or go out is "Early" or "Late." His common movements, the smallest events of his day, are secret.

Mother follows these like a female detective. "Kenyon left the bread out this morning and the pimento cheese. I wonder if he had pimento cheese for breakfast, or took sandwiches for lunch, or both?" If, after she counts the remaining bread slices, sandwiches seem a possibility, she wonders where he has to go that's so distant he needs to take lunch with him. The names of surrounding towns come to her mind. "He won't be going anywhere near Lampasas because they have good barbeque there and he wouldn't take pimento cheese if he could get barbeque." She has advantage over Daddy; at least she's observed Kenyon's eating habits through the years and can spend hours happily trying to guess what he's going to do about lunch and whether or not he's going to turn up for supper.

Daddy doesn't care about where Kenyon eats lunch. What he wants to know is how many ranches Kenyon is leasing, how his sheep, goats, and cattle are doing, if he's making money or not.

We all want to know if he's ever going to get married. Does he have a girl? Does he want to marry? He is almost thirty, taller than my father's six feet, though how much we don't know for he won't stand and be measured. He has dark hair that curls when he forgets to get it cut, which is most of the time. The curls come over his forehead and disgust him so much he is forever jamming his hat down low to cover his hair. When we were children he made me cut the front curls off. I was spanked for doing it. His nose is long and straight. There is a small slanting scar just missing his eye running over his left eyebrow. His eyes are brown. His mouth is wide and generally closed.

When we ask if he's ever going to marry, and nothing will stop us from asking, he says, "Find me a girl who'll live out in the country, cook beans, and wash all day." He runs his hands over the creases in his clean blue jeans, sticks the shirttail of his clean shirt in, and laughs. Mother gets angry then. She's responsible for all his clean clothes and feels sometimes this is the only reason he shows up at the house. Often she says, "He doesn't need a wife! He needs a washerwoman!" Not once, however, has she ever said this to him, fearing he'll put on his boots and walk out the door to some unknown cafe one last time.

She isn't curious about where I'm going to eat. Everybody in town knows I each lunch every day at the Leon High School cafeteria. I'm the singing teacher. Wouldn't you know it! Since I've already told you Kenyon's almost thirty, you might as well know I'm almost twenty-six. At least nobody asks me when I'm going to get married, not to my face anyway. Being related and having practically no heart at all, Kenyon has the gall to wonder out loud if I'm ever going to catch a man. When he does this, I tell him I have as much right to uphold the long tradition of old-maidhood as he has to represent the last of the old west. My brother is a cowboy.

I tell him, "You're the last of a vanishing breed, the tail end of the roundup of the longhorn steers, the last great auk alive, a prairie rooster without a hen!"

All he replies to this is, "Sister, there ain't no substitute for beef on the hoof." He gets out real quick before I can go on about helicopters substituting for horses and feed lots replacing the open range.

Since the wires have been cut between Kenyon and his family, we have to depend on other sources of information, the weekly newspaper for instance. That's where we found out he'd been riding bulls in rodeos the summer after he flunked out of college. He got his picture on the front page for falling off a Brahma bull headfirst. The photographer caught the bull still doubled up and Kenyon in midair, his hands out in front of him right before he hit the dirt. My daddy strictly forbade any more bull-riding on the grounds he wasn't going to have his son associating with a bunch of rodeo bums.

Kenyon said, "These bums are the best friends I got and I'll associate with whoever I want."

"You are going to kill yourself and me too." Daddy put his hand over his heart like he was going to have an attack that minute. "And, furthermore, I'm going to cut you out of my will if you keep up this fool riding." Then he laid down on the bed and made me take his blood pressure. I was home on vacation from nursing school in Galveston.

Kenyon smiled, showing he still had all his teeth, and the next thing we read in the newspaper was he'd gone off and joined the paratroopers, joined of his own free will, mind you, for three years. Daddy, who'd been in the infantry in WW II, was half proud and half wild. "He doesn't have enough sense to keep his feet on the ground! If he isn't being thrown from a bull, he's throwing himself out of airplanes!" He wrote an old army buddy of his who'd retired, like he did, near his last post—except the post was up in Tennessee where Kenyon was stationed instead of Texas where we are. This old buddy wrote back saying:

Dear Willie,

Your boy is doing fine. I talked to his C.O. yesterday. He told me Pvt. Kenyon K. Lane is making a good soldier.

Yours truly,

Henry C. Worth, Lt. Col., Ret.

P.S. He told me Kenyon inspires good morale because he jumps out of planes with a wad of tobacco in his mouth and spits all the way down.

Your friend,
Lt. Col. Henry C. Worth, Ret.

I think Daddy was happy for a while. He showed the letter to me before he went downtown to show it to some of his friends at the drugstore where they all meet for coffee. By the time he came home, Mother was back from the grocery.

"William, how can you go around showing everybody that letter when I haven't read it!" She read it and was crying before she finished. "Who taught him how to chew tobacco? He'll ruin his teeth. He was such a nice clean boy."

"Ruin his teeth!" Daddy shouted. "You've got to worry about his teeth when he's falling out of airplanes every day!"

"He's not falling," I said. "He's jumping and he's doing it of his own free will."

"Free will nothing!" Daddy turned on me. "Don't you be telling me about free will in the U.S. Army. I know about the army. I spent twenty years in the army."

I had to take his blood pressure after that. He spent the next three years writing to his army buddies near whatever post my brother happened to be on, and getting news of Kenyon from them. All his letters were signed Col. William K. Lane, Ret.

I spent those years finishing my education, they thought. In the daytime I was. I wore a white uniform and low white shoes and went to nursing school in Galveston. Friday and Saturday nights I put on a red sequined dress and a pair of red high heels and went to sing at one of the nightclubs. My stage name was Gabriella and I wore so much makeup nobody from Leon would have known it was me. I had learned something from Kenyon, not to tell everything I knew and to follow my own free will. It worked too. When I was home I took Daddy's blood pressure and Mother's temperature; when I was in Galveston I was singing two nights a week.

Don't get any ideas either—singing and wearing a red dress was all I was doing. The men in the combo I sang with were more strict

with me than they would have been with their own daughters if they
had had any. I could drink soda pop only, and I had to sit with one
of them while I was drinking. Except for the sequins I might as well
have been in a convent. I sang songs like "I Can't Say No" without
ever having a chance to not say it. Still, I was satisfied. Singing was
what I wanted. I thought if I could support myself by nursing, I
could gradually work my way into show biz and up to New York. So
I was down in Galveston nursing and singing while my brother was
on some army post jumping out of airplanes, I supposed.

One Friday night I was giving out with "Zip-Pah-De-Do-Dah"
trying to cheer up a few barflies when in walks Kenyon. He knows
me right away, red sequins, makeup, and all. He is wearing a tight-
fitting paratrooper's uniform, his pants tied up in his boots, which
laced to the knee practically. Very spiffy and clean. Mother would
have been happy to see him.

"My, oh, my, what a wonderful day!" I finish. The barflies ap-
plaud. My brother just stands quietly while I slink off the platform.
It's time for the break, so Tiny the drummer, who is actually a big
fat man, married with a wife and baby he calls every night in Dallas,
takes me by the arm to a table. Kenyon comes right over. I can see
immediately he has gotten himself all shined up for one reason—to
get roaring drunk—to the disgrace of family and country. He's just
off the reservation and ready to howl. Obviously, I'm in his way.

I smile at him and say, "Hi. What are you doing down here? Are
you AWOL?"

"No," he grins, "I'm on leave. You're the one that's AWOL."

Tiny says, "Scram, soldier boy."

"It's my brother, Tiny. He's in the paratroopers. He jumps out of
airplanes."

"Gay Baby, don't pull the brother bit on me."

"But he is," I insist. "Show him your birthmark or something,
Kenyon."

"Jump on out of here, fly boy," says Tiny.

"If I go, you go too, Gay Baby," says Kenyon with a merciless
smirk.

"I'm not going anywhere till I finish here tonight. You sit down and behave yourself. Have a beer."

"You're leaving right now. My sister isn't going to hang around no honky-tonk." With this he grabs me by the arm and I scream at him, "Let go!" But he doesn't and by this time I'm furious. "You auk! You dodo! You idiot!"

Tiny rises like a giant blimp slowly filling with air. Before he can signal to the other fellows though, Kenyon pulls me to my feet. The other four members of the combo—Louie, the piano player; Max, the bass; Joe, the sax; and Evans, the trumpet—run to assist us.

Kenyon turns the table on its side. "She's going with me," he says.

I peek between the fingers of my free hand to see if he's got a six-shooter in his free hand. He's got nothing, nothing but swagger. Pretty soon he has a cut over his left eye—Tiny did it with a chair—and I have not one red cent left of all my savings from singing nights. My going-to-New York money has gone to bail Dangerous Dan Kenyon McGrew out of the Galveston jail.

"Listen, Kenyon," I tell him, "this is not Leon and this is not the nineteenth century. It's the second half of the twentieth in case you haven't noticed it from your airplane riding! There is nothing wrong with me singing in a quiet respectable bar."

"No sister of mine—"

"You just pretend I'm not any sister of yours. We're so different one of us must have been left on the doorstep."

"You think I'm a bastard?"

"Well, you're the one calling the cards," I said and flounced out of the jail. I was mad and in a hurry to get home to bed. All I cared about right then was sleep. That particular Saturday I had to work the 7:00 A.M. shift at the hospital. Kenyon being such a zipper-lip type, I certainly wasn't worrying about him telling anybody I was working in a nightclub and him spending some time in jail. I should have let him stay in jail. He got in his car that very same night and drove straight to Leon. And, when he got there early the next morning, he told. He told everything he knew.

They didn't give me any warning, not a phone call—nothing. Daddy appeared in full uniform, the old army pinks and greens with eagles flapping on both shoulders. He had been getting ready to leave for a battalion reunion at Ft. Sam Houston when Kenyon showed up, and he didn't waste time changing clothes. He should have. His stomach had expanded some since WW II so his trousers were lifted an inch too high over his socks.

The first thing I said when I saw him was, "Daddy, what on earth are you doing down here in your uniform? It's non-reg. They don't wear that kind anymore."

"Sister, don't you tell me about the U.S. Army regulations. I gave twenty years of my life to them."

"Well, they are likely to slap you in the loony bin here for walking around dressed up like that."

"If I was you, I wouldn't be talking about how other people are dressed."

"Daddy, there is nothing wrong with my uniform," I said. I'd been wearing it for eight hours and hadn't spilt a thing on it. There was nothing wrong with the way I looked at all except for the circles under my eyes from staying up till 2:00 A.M. getting a certain person out of jail. I was just about dead from exhaustion.

"I hear you've got another dress, a red one."

We were talking in the lobby of the hospital and when he said that I wanted to call for a stretcher.

"No daughter of mine is going to hang around with gangsters at nightclubs."

I don't know where he got the gangsters, probably from the last time he was in a nightclub.

"This isn't 1920 and I don't know any gangsters. The fellows Kenyon got in a fight with are musicians. They were trying to protect me." He wasn't listening. He didn't want to hear my side. His mind was already made up.

"You go and get your things," he told me. "No daughter of mine is going to be corrupted by jazz and booze."

What could I do? I'd spent all my savings getting Kenyon out of jail. I went with Daddy back to Leon thinking it would all blow over after a while. Mother, at least, would be on my side since she knew what it was to live with a husband who still thought he was in the first half of the twentieth century and a son who hadn't progressed past 1900. When we got to Leon though, I found out different. The very first thing Mother did was to show me mine and Kenyon's birth certificates.

"Look here, young lady, neither you nor your brother was left on anybody's doorstep. I hope this is proof enough for you." She shoved the yellowed pages with their loopy-de-loop handwriting in my face and started crying before I could say I never really meant it.

I stayed home that weekend and the rest of that semester. Goodbye nursing. I wasn't so crazy about it anyway. I guess what happened to me could happen to anybody, but I wonder how many girls end up teaching a bunch of high school kids to sing "Sweet Adeline" after they started out with a great career in show biz. Daddy took me completely out of school. In January he let me enroll in a Baptist church college only forty miles from Leon. I got my teacher's certificate there in music education and that's all I got. They had a short rope on me.

When I finished I was twenty-three, due to the interruption in my education. Daddy had a heart attack that year and I went home to help Mother nurse him and to teach singing in Leon High School.

My brother, when he was through with the paratroopers, came home too. He started working on ranches and slowly saved enough to lease places of his own. He hadn't paid me back the bail money yet. I hadn't paid him back either, but I was planning on how I was going to. Someday, I thought, he is going to find some girl who wants to quit riding the barrel races in rodeos and get married. When he brings this cutie home in her embroidered blouse and her buckskin fringes, I am going to tell everything I know, not about him being in jail. The fact he spent a few hours in the Galveston jail wouldn't bother her. Galveston's a long way from Leon.

I wasn't going to tell this rodeo queen Kenyon was bound to drag home about his past; I was going to predict her future. I was going to let this little girl know she might as well throw away her western breeches and get into a skirt that hit the floor. And, I was going to tell her she'd better wave goodbye forever to the bright lights, the crowd, the band, and the Grand Entry Parade because all that was in store for her was a pot of beans to stir and blue jeans to wash at home on the range. She wasn't to expect any modern appliances to help her out either, because I knew Kenyon. He wouldn't buy her a single machine, not even a radio. If she wanted to hear any music she'd have to invite me out to sit on the front porch and sing "Zip-Pah-De-Do-Dah" as the sun sank slowly in the west.

I had it all planned out, a feeble sort of revenge, but at least I'd have my say—me, the Cassandra of Leon, prophesying a terrible future for a fun-loving cowboy's sweetheart. Of course, like a lot of too well planned revenges, it didn't turn out that way. I got restless sitting around in the teacher's lounge, going to the movie every Saturday night with a man I'd known since we were both in high school, Alvin Neeley, the band director. We weren't anything to each other but companions in boredom, chained together by what everyone thought was our common interest, music. We were supposed to be a perfect couple because we could both read notes. Everyone imagined we were sitting on the piano bench warbling duets, but we weren't.

Alvin was a marcher. He kept in step even when we were walking a few blocks down the street, and believe me, he wasn't marching to the sound of any distant drum. Alvin had his own drum in his head, and when he puckered his lips, I knew he wasn't puckering up for me; he was puckering up for Sousa. Sometimes, just for diversion, I'd refuse to march in step with him. If he put his left foot forward, I'd start out on my right, but he'd always notice and with a quick little skip in the air, he'd be in step with me. Off we'd go marching to the movie to the tune of "The Stars and Stripes Forever" every Saturday. And all this time Kenyon was stomping in and out of the house bird-free, intent on his own secret purposes.

Mother would come and sit on the foot of my bed after I got home from a date with Alvin. "Did you have a good time?" she'd say.

"All right." I wasn't going to tell her I'd had a bad time. She had enough troubles as it was. Since his heart attack my daddy spent most of his time sitting around the house with his right hand on the left side of his chest the way actors used to indicate great pain in the old silent films.

She'd ask me what movie we saw and I'd tell her, *Monsters of the Slimy Green Deep* or whatever it was. Nothing but Grade B movies ever made it to Leon, and Alvin and I went regularly no matter what was showing—like taking a pill on schedule.

"Well, how is Alvin getting along?"

She wasn't interested in Alvin's health. What she wanted to know was how Alvin and I were getting along. I'd say all right to that too. I kept on saying the same thing till one night she said, "I sure would like to have some grandchildren."

"Mother, you better get Kenyon to work on that because you're not going to get any grandchildren out of me and Alvin Neeley."

"Why not?"

"I'd have to marry him—that's why, and I'm not going to even if he asks, and he's not going to ask. He can barely hold a conversation anyway. All he can do is whistle—and march." I was sitting across the room from her rubbing my aching legs.

"Why do you keep on going out with him then?"

"I don't see anybody else bashing the door down to ask me to a movie. I go out with Alvin because he takes me. It's one way of getting away from this house, a way of getting out of Leon even if it's to go to the *Slimy Green Deep*."

"You worry me," said Mother.

"I worry myself," I told her and I did. I was stuck with Alvin Neeley in Leon. I'd done what they all wanted me to do and now they were stuck with me. They had me on their hands.

Mother evidently spoke to Kenyon about my miserable unwed existence and insisted he find somebody for me. I say Mother did it, put the idea in Kenyon's head that he find somebody for me, because, left to himself, Kenyon was not at all bothered by an old-maid sister. He thought he'd saved me from the gutter. From there on I was supposed to be continually thankful and permanently respectable.

When I got home early one Saturday night I was told, before I had time to say anything, that he'd "fixed up" a date for me the following Saturday.

"Who with?"

"Fellow named Frank Harwell from Lampasas. He ranches out west of town. He's going to take you dancing."

"He's from a big family. I know some of them. Harwells are spread all over Lampasas," Mother said happily.

"He served in Korea, in the infantry," said Daddy as if he'd just pinned the Distinguished Conduct Medal on somebody.

They all knew what they wanted to know about Frank Harwell and I didn't know a thing. "How old is he? Is he short or tall, skinny or fat, intelligent or ignorant, handsome or ugly?" I could have gone on all night throwing questions at them, but I quit. They were all sitting there looking so smug.

"He's the best I could do," said Kenyon. "You'll like him. All the girls do."

"Where are we going dancing?" Since Leon's in a dry county there's not a real nightclub within twenty miles.

"We'll go out to the VFW Club," Kenyon said.

"We? Are you going too? Who do you have a date with?"

"Nobody. I'm just going along for the ride."

"Kenyon, I'm twenty-five years old going on twenty-six, and I'll be damned if you're going anywhere as my chaperone."

"Sister, watch your language," said Daddy. "Is he a good dancer, Kenyon?"

"Daddy, what do you care if he's a good dancer or not? You're not the one who's going to be dancing with him."

"I don't want my daughter marrying some Valentino. Good dancers make bad husbands."

"Daddy! You are hopelessly behind times! If you'd turn on your TV set you'd see people dancing without even touching each other. The Valentinos are all gone. Anyway, I'm not going to my wedding Saturday night. I'm going to the VFW Club!"

They had me. I was trapped into having a date with Frank Harwell just to prove to Daddy he wasn't a Valentino. I didn't mind so much. After all, I'd endured a long dry march in the desert with Alvin Neeley. And, I wanted to know what Kenyon did with himself when he wasn't riding the range.

On Saturday night I pranced into the living room in my best and fullest skirt. You have to have plenty of leg room for country dances. Kenyon was standing talking to Frank Harwell, who looked like a cowboy straight out of a cigarette advertisement, lean, tanned, and terribly sure of himself. He was every young girl's dream, and old girl's too. My knees were shaking a little when he looked me over. For a minute I wished I hadn't worn a sensible dress. I wished I was all togged out in my red sequins and red high heels again.

We all three got in Frank's pickup. He and Kenyon did most of the talking. We hadn't gone two blocks before Kenyon insisted he had to stop and look at some stock at the auction barn on the way to the VFW.

"Fine," said Frank in a grand, easy-going way. He was the most totally relaxed man I'd ever seen. He drove his pickup through town with one hand on the wheel, guiding it to the right and left as if he were reining a horse.

When we got to the auction barn Kenyon shot out of the truck, leaving the door open behind him.

"Always in a hurry," said Frank and leaned over me to pull the door shut. I felt like a huge old cat had fallen in my lap.

"You don't seem to be."

"Naw." He eased himself up, pulled out a package of cigarettes, lit one, then leaned back and blew smoke out. I kept expecting to hear an announcer's voice saying something about how good cigarettes were so I waited a minute before saying anything myself. Finally, I asked him about his ranch. He told me about his spring round-up, how much mohair had been clipped from his goats, how many cows had calved, the number of rattlesnakes he'd killed, how much a good rain would help, and other interesting things like that. We sat there, with Frank worrying about his wells running dry and the miles of fence he needed to repair; I was worrying about whether we'd ever get to the dance. The VFW Club was on top of a hill behind the auction barn. We could have walked up there, but it could have been in the next county as far as Frank was concerned. He got a bottle of bourbon out of the glove compartment and took a long swallow from it. When Kenyon came back he passed the bottle to him. Neither one of them offered me a swallow and I knew I'd have to be seventy and taking whiskey for medicinal purposes before either one of those two would dream of offering a girl a drink.

Kenyon was excited about a bull he'd seen. "He's that same old Brahma that throwed me. I'd know him anywhere. Gentle as he can be outside the ring, but let somebody get on his back and he goes wild. Wonder why they're selling him. He's a good rodeo bull."

"Getting old maybe," Frank drawled. They both laughed as if he'd said the most hilarious thing in the world. Then they both took another drink so *they* were in a good mood when we got to the VFW at 9:30 P.M. The hall was an old WW II army surplus barracks the veterans had bought and painted white. Judging from the noise coming out of the place, the men standing around cars outside talking and sneaking drinks, and the two cops at the doorway, it was wilder than any Galveston club on a Saturday night. The cops nodded at us as we went in. The girl who was selling tickets to the dance warned Frank and Kenyon to hold on to them because nobody was allowed to come back in without one.

Frank swung me out on the dance floor and that was the last I saw of Kenyon for a while except for a glimpse of him out of the corner of my eye. He was dancing with one of my ex-students, a not so bright one, who'd somehow managed to graduate the year before. Every once in a while Frank would excuse himself to go out and take a swig from his bottle. I sat at a table by myself drinking soda pop and thinking about my Galveston days when I at least had the company of some grown men when I was drinking. The musicians at the VFW that night, by the way, hardly deserved the name. They sawed and wheezed through their whole repertory which consisted of about fifteen songs, all sounding alike. It's fashionable now to like what everyone calls "country music," but if you had to sit out in the VFW and listen to it, you'd get pretty tired of the music and the country.

After a while I caught sight of Frank strolling in the front door. He stopped by another table for a minute to pat a girl on the top of her frizzy blonde head, then he ambled on over to me.

"Where's Kenyon?" I was tired of listening to the whining songs, tired of being flung around the dance floor. The new dances I'd told Daddy about hadn't gotten to Leon yet—they probably never will get to Frank Harwell. The more he drank the harder he danced, not on my toes, but stomping hard on the floor taking great wide steps and swinging me around in circles. It was 1:00 A.M., time to go home. Nobody else seemed to think so though. The hall was even more packed than when we first came in.

"Last time I saw him Kenyon was outside arguing with the cops. He's lost his ticket and they won't let him back in."

"Why doesn't he buy another one?"

"He thinks they ought to take his word he already bought one. You know he's got high principles and—"

"I know about his principles all right. He's got high principles and no scruples!!"

"Aw, don't be too hard on your brother."

I was getting ready to tell him that Kenyon had been hard on me when we both turned our heads to see what was causing all the shouting down by the door. It was my brother leading that gentle old Brahma bull by a rope around his neck. The crowd was parting before him. Some of them were jumping out the windows and everybody else was headed for the back door. The blonde Frank had patted on the head was standing on top of a table screaming, "Help! Somebody do something!" Nobody was doing anything but getting out. Kenyon staggered through the hall with a mean grin on his face, drunk as the lord of the wild frontier and cool as a walking ice cube. Behind the bandstand the musicians were crawling out the windows. The bass fiddler tried to throw his fiddle out first, but it got stuck. He left it there, half in, half out, and wriggled through another window. A man following him didn't watch where he was going and caught his foot in the middle of a drum.

Behind Kenyon the bull, uncertain of his footing on the slippery floor, was trying to adjust himself. He slid along, his tail lashing frantically, his hooves skidding in all directions. When Kenyon slowed down a little to get past some tables the Brahma snorted and jumped—like Alvin Neeley doing his little skip in mid-air to keep in step.

"Come on. We can't stand here gawking. Somebody's going to get hurt if Kenyon lets that old bull go." Frank grabbed my hand and we headed for the back door. By the time we got out Kenyon and the bull had the VFW Club to themselves.

We waited out back. The cops waited too. Kenyon appeared in the doorway. The bull nudged up behind him. He turned and scratched the bull's head.

"I told you," Kenyon hollered at the cops, "I already bought one ticket." Then he walked down the steps carefully leading the bull, talking to him all the way. "Watch your step, old buddy. That's right. Easy now."

The cops let Kenyon put the bull back in the auction pen, and when he was finished, they put him in their car. He was laughing so hard he couldn't fight very well, but he tried.

"Oh Lord!" Frank sighed lazily from the safety of his pickup. "If he wouldn't fight, they'd let him go. Those boys were ready for that dance to break up anyway."

"Aren't you going to help him?"

"Naw. He took this on hisself. You want us both in jail?"

"In jail?"

"Yeah," Frank drawled and hoisted his big handsome self across the seat toward me.

"Shouldn't we follow them?"

"Look at that moon."

There wasn't a moon in sight, not a sliver of one. Gorgeous Frank Harwell was so sleepy drunk he mistook somebody's headlights for the moon. All the excitement on top of all the dancing we'd done was too much for him I guess, because the next thing I knew he'd passed out. I lifted his head off my shoulder, propped it up against the window, and climbed into the driver's seat.

I got to the jail in time to hear them book Kenyon for being drunk and disorderly and disturbing the peace. He paid his own way out this time, but the only reason they didn't lock him up for the night was I was there to take him home. Of course, I couldn't take him home in his condition. Daddy would have had an attack and Mother would have probably fainted at the sight of him. Her clean-cut, hard-working, tight-lipped boy was a living mess. He looked like he'd been riding the bull rather than leading him. I managed to brush most of the dust off of him. The cops gave him back his hat. We stopped at Leon's one open-all-night cafe, where I went in and got a quart of black coffee. When he'd finished this he was sober enough to go in the men's room and wash his face. Frank slept through the whole rehabilitation.

Kenyon wanted to park the pickup on the square across from the jail and walk home, leaving Frank there snoring. "Maybe the cops will come out and get him," he said.

"It's not any use to get mad at Frank. It was your idea to bring that animal into the dance hall."

"You taking up for him?"

"I got you out of jail, didn't I?"

Kenyon nodded. I went in the cafe to get some more coffee for Frank. When I came back out Kenyon started shaking him, but before he got him awake he turned to me and said, "Sister, don't tell everything you know."

"Why not? Mother and Daddy are going to find out anyway. By church time tomorrow everybody in town will be talking—"

"I'd rather they get it second-hand."

By this time I was so mad I jabbed Frank with my elbow, handed him the coffee, and lit into Kenyon. "You'd rather everybody get everything second-hand. Nobody is supposed to do anything but you."

"What are you talking about?"

"Never mind! You wouldn't understand if I kept talking till sun-up, but I'll tell you this, Kenyon—I'm not going to devote the rest of my life to keeping you out of jail. From now on you are on your own."

"Sister, I've always been on my own."

How contrary can a person be? Here I'd just saved him from a night in the Leon County jail, not to mention the time I got him out of the Galveston jail. I didn't argue with him though. I knew if I told him he wasn't on his own till he left home, he wouldn't wait a minute before telling me the same thing—with Frank Harwell sitting right next to me taking in every word.

"You want me to drive?" Kenyon asked him.

"Naw, you have got in enough trouble tonight, you and that dancing bull. I'll make it."

They both laughed. Frank even tried to slap my knee, but I dodged him.

"I want to go home," I said.

"Gal, that's where we're going."

It was 2:30 A.M. I could imagine Daddy sitting on the front porch wrapped in his overcoat with his M-1 stretched across his knees. For once, we were lucky. Mother and Daddy were both in bed asleep. Kenyon and I tiptoed to our rooms without waking either one of them. When they asked us the next morning where we'd been so late, Kenyon said, "Dancing." Since they were used to short answers from him he didn't have to say anything else. Of course Mother came and sat on the foot of my bed and asked me all about Frank Harwell.

"Mother, Frank is a very handsome man and no doubt all the other girls like him, but he is a cowboy and I think one cowboy is enough in the family."

Then I told her. "In June I'm going down to San Antonio and look for a job in one of the schools there."

"You can't—"

"Yes, I can. If I don't leave home now, I'll be right here the rest of my days."

"She might as well," Kenyon said. He was leaning in the doorway, eavesdropping to see whether I was going to tell on him. "She's too uppity for anybody in Leon." With that he turned around and left. He didn't know it, but it was the best thing he could have said. Daddy blamed himself for giving me too much education and Mother was so anxious to be a grandmother I think she'd have been happy to see me off to New York.

In June I went to San Antonio and found a job at one of the high schools. I found a husband, too, a fine doctor who sings in the chorus during opera season. That's where I met him—in the chorus. We were rehearsing for *La Traviata*. His name is Edward Greenlee. Dr. Edward Greenlee.

"Can he rope?" Kenyon asked.

"Can you tie a suture?"

"What branch of the army was he in?"

"He was in the navy, Daddy."

"Is he from a large family?"

"Mother, there are Greenlees all over San Antonio."

We had a June wedding in the First Methodist in Leon. Daddy gave me away. Kenyon was an usher. He looked handsome in his white tux jacket, the only one he'd ever worn in his life. I told him so when I got to the church in my bridal finery. He said thanks and grinned his tight-lipped grin. I looked down. The black pants covered all of the stitching decorating the tops, but I could plainly see, and so could everybody else at my wedding, that Kenyon had his boots on.

I guess he'll go on being true to the code and die with them on. He's living out on one of his ranches now, fifteen miles from the nearest town and ninety miles from San Antonio. Sometimes on Sunday afternoons Edward and I take the children and drive up to see him. There's no way of letting him know we're coming because he doesn't have a telephone. We don't have to worry about inconveniencing anybody though; Kenyon lives by himself.

The last time we were there we missed him. My five-year-old boy, William, walked around on the bare floors and said, "Doesn't he have any rugs?"

When we were checking the cupboards in the almost bare kitchen Cynthia, our three-year-old, wailed, "Doesn't he have any cookies?"

"No, he doesn't have any rugs and he doesn't have any cookies. But he does have a bathtub, hot and cold running water, a bed, a fire, three cans of chili, a sack of flour, two horses, a sheep dog, and a whole lot of sheep, goats, and cattle."

"Why doesn't he have any cookies?"

"This sure is a lumpy old chair," said William. He should have known. He was sitting in the only one in the room. "Is Uncle Kenyon poor?"

"All of your Uncle Kenyon's money is tied up in stock, the sheep, and goats and cattle," said Edward, who always tries to explain things.

"Uncle Kenyon is a cowboy," I said, which was really the only explanation.

In Captivity

Ruth, half listening, holds the receiver away from her ear trying to keep her sister's noise muted like a distant ambulance or fire siren, a moan to be cancelled out since there is nothing she can do about it.

"I don't know what they want." Louise, thousands of miles to the north, wails into the telephone, and Ruth, who has heard the complaint many times, wonders if the wires carrying her voice quiver and sigh with the sound of it. "They" are her daughter Karen and Danel, the boy she is determined to marry. They are also all long-haired, embroidery-patched young lovers of the good earth, health foods, and pot. Ruth is supposed to be an expert on them because they are her students. She is weary of being considered an expert. Now, toward the end of the semester, she is particularly tired of her sister's relentless interest in the generation gap. The words, so worn with use, are frayed at the edges like this year's blue jeans, a fad so heavily exploited it is no longer remarkable. Mothers of children, what did you expect? Unless they rebel, they can't grow up. Go to Europe, Louise. Take a trip yak-back through the Himalayas, sail off to the South Pole in a balloon, do high deeds in the Andes, do anything. Leave Karen and Danel alone. She wishes her the luck of the four winds and seven seas, yet only says laconically, "Worry about your own life. They'll take care of theirs."

"But what about his hair? Can you get him to cut it? I can put up with it, but Mother—"

"He's not going to live with you or Mother. I'm sick of the hair question. It's not a reliable standard." She starts to tell her you can't judge a person by the length of his hair any more than the Elizabethans could judge a man's virility by the size of his codpiece, but she doesn't extend the argument to the Elizabethans. Louise would only put the whole point down to a scholarly old maid's interest in sex. True, she is now thirty-eight. Louise persists in believing in the maiden and Ruth lets her as she can see no sense in attempting to explain her life to her married sister. If she told her anything about Murray, Louise would press for marriage without ever seeing him, without knowing anything about him. The usual questions would be asked: Who is he? What does he do? How old is he? As soon as the answers were given—he's divorced, a prof in the government department, about forty—Louise would pounce. She belonged to a family of pouncers. If sheer will could marry anyone, they would have married her off in an instant. Their parents had only two daughters and all daughters ought to marry. Having vowed never to get desperate about marriage—she is certain happiness is not solely dependent upon being married or single—she fights her family's desperation with silence.

Hooking her heels a rung higher on the phone booth's stool, Ruth waves through the glass-panelled door to one of her ex-students, Jack . . . bearded, beaded, and barefooted. He cannot walk into any restaurant in town, even washaterias won't have him unless he puts on shoes, but he can wander the corridors of university buildings safely all day long.

"I want you to tell her she shouldn't—"

"I know what you want, and I told you when Karen came down to Texas it was impossible. I can't monitor her daily here any more than you can in New York. Please quit worrying. I've got a class to teach in five minutes."

"I can't help but worry. Mother called me this morning. It's funny. I told her almost the same thing you're telling me."

"Who started Mother up again? Aunt Judith?"

"Yes, of course, who else?" Aunt Judith has been the family gossip monger all their lives. They both laugh. Mother lives in Georgia. They have escaped the interwoven net of family ties only to be threaded in again by telephone lines.

"Louise, I really have to go." She puts the receiver down with one hand and pushes the door open with the other. Though this is the new wing of the building, no improvement has been made on phone booths. As in the old wing, they are locked. Only faculty members have keys to them, a ridiculous form of privilege. She is forever loaning her key to students. As she comes out she stretches both arms over her head. Boxes with locks give her a mild form of claustrophobia even though she's not a large woman; she is slight. Her thinness is so accentuated by a preference for tailored clothes that she sometimes looks on her body as a composition of awkward angles. Murray assures her he likes her angles, but she mistrusts assurance of this kind; in bed praise is easily given. Out of bed? He tells her she is a good cook. True, she likes to eat, likes cooking for Murray, but cooking is simply a time-consuming skill she has acquired from her mother. All talk about food bores her. If anyone asks her for recipes, particularly those who admire something as simple as coq au vin, she answers with a mixture of nonsense partially imagined, partially taken from old Southern cookbooks. First you skin the possum, then you put him in a bucket of ice water on top of the roof overnight. Bash six green onions gathered at first shine during the second quarter of the full moon with a silver knife inherited from your great-uncle . . . Julia Troll, Murray calls her. Julia Trull, Ruthie Ravenous, Rowdy Ruth.

She returns to her office, her cave in the English department, underground on floor B for Bottom. It cannot be B for Basement for no one in Texas has a basement, something her parents talk about every time they come to visit. Yes, we have no basements in Texas she hums to the tune of "Yes, We Have No Bananas." It's one of the few things she can agree with them about. She faces two windows looking out onto a blank cement wall. An air shaft outside at ground level lets light filter in. She's thought of getting an artist to paint a mural on the wall, one with vast receding distances, but now is not the Renaissance and she is no Medici. She is a proficient liar though. Her classes have already met. It is almost time for office hours to begin. She would rather be outside, where Karen is probably leading a songfest at the base of the statue of George Washington rampant. He is posed standing, cloak furled behind him, but the Italian sculptor hadn't been able to carry out the D.A.R.'s deepest wishes. Contrary to all historical possibility, they wanted a founding father rooted firmly to Texas soil. In part they got him. The jaw is determined, his face noble, mouth clamped shut. However, his feet, though close to the ground, are placed one in front of the other. He appears poised to take off striding down the grassy mall in front of him, his cloak waving in the wind, away from it all. Ruth watches with pleasure as he walks past all the other statues: Albert Sidney Johnston and Robert E. Lee on his right, and on his left Governor Hogg, the big-bellied governor of Texas in the '90s. He is balked at Littlefield Fountain, a writhing conglomerate of allegorical hash, left by a repentant Confederate officer as a memorial to the reunion of the states after the Civil War. G.W. walks around Columbia, the army and navy in various semiclassical stages of nudity, pauses to wonder how Neptune's horses got hitched to the ship of state, and wades on through the descending pools as Karen and other students did in the days before $100 fines were set for waders. Ruth loses sight of G.W. at this point. She feels he'll go straight on to the capitol building, which looks rather like the national capitol, and demand to know what the hell the country is coming to.

Her daydreams are often spent in such fantasies, covert rebellions against being held forever in one stance or pacing within thick lines of daily routines and the boundaries of her own inadequacies. Escape, yes, but to what? What if she quit teaching? How could she escape her own love of learning or her tendency to attract the wrong kind of men? Like a miser counting her losses, she listed them: Robert was weak, Tom too domineering. Marshall too young and too confused about himself to be truly interested in anyone else. Murray . . . just around. That was all, a presence. What did Karen hope for when she fell in love with Danel? Nothing, probably. It had happened as accidentally as the peculiar spelling of his name.

"That's the way Daniel sounded to his mother," Karen said with obvious pride in the simplicity of ignorance.

"What's his last name?"

"H-u-g-h-e-s."

Amused by the contrariness of people's minds, Ruth smiled. Then she remembered the boy. Long blonde hair, an angelic face, sat in the middle of the second or third row, wrote one short paper—passable, but full of convoluted sentences stuffed with academic jargon. She'd given him a C and a warning about the snares of language. He was absent for weeks after, came in to get the assignment for his second paper, and vanished. What happened to him? What became of students like Danel, those that faded away? They didn't always leave school. The next semester when she was driving along a street near the university she saw him loping down the sidewalk. If she hadn't been in the wrong lane of traffic, she would have jumped out of her car and asked him where he'd been, but not because she was vindictive, only curious.

Karen was watching her, reading her face for signs of unfavorable reaction as she usually did, waiting for somebody to say no, wanting it said maybe, looking for lines to step over. Well, she had provided some: she'd refused to taxi Karen and her friends home from various rallies that didn't break up till 2 A.M., refused to try to talk Louise into letting her have a motorcycle, refused all invitations to drug experiences, refused the use of her house for pot parties. In return she was pushed into accepting the fact she had become an unwilling member of the establishment, another tiresome pigeonhole she detested being put into. It was like becoming a grandmother at twenty. Louise had already made her an aunt at twelve—aunt of a child who grew up writing poetry, studying music, studying everything. Mothers of children, how do you do it? How did Louise and Tom, both normally intelligent, produce such a child? Over-bright, nervous, quick, Karen's rounded owl-eyes, rounded more by circular wire-rimmed glasses, stared at her.

"What ever happened to him?"

"He dropped out that semester. He said you encouraged him in a way."

"I did?"

"He was all tied up in papers and things—going in circles, could hardly make sense of what he was doing. You told him so yourself."

"I did? Perhaps— One bad paper is no reason for—"

"It was one of a series. You were the only teacher who told him exactly what was wrong. He already knew it in a way, but you confirmed it. Danel didn't really want to be an English major anyway. He doesn't want a degree now. He worked for a while as a zookeeper in San Antonio. That's what he wants—to work with animals. He quit though. He says they mistreat the animals there. The cages are too small and—"

"What's he doing now?"

"Oh, he's just around. He's got a job as a busboy in a cafe. He's been living with me kind of . . . He's got a truck."

"How can he live in a truck?"

"It's an old milk truck."

"Oh." Ruth was silent for a long minute trying to understand why living in a milk truck explained anything.

"He started living with me this fall. Look, Ruth, I met him. He had this truck and needed someplace in town— He used to park it out in the country, but he had to move in to get closer to work. There was nothing in the garage over at my place."

"So that's why the garage door is always shut. What does your landlady think about a milk truck in the garage?"

"She never comes around. I mail the rent to an agency here. Danel helps with it when he can. Busboys don't get paid much."

There was a long silence. Ruth waited it out.

"We want to get married. I'm going to tell Mother and Dad Thanksgiving." Karen smiled the secret, placid smile of a woman who's arrived at a decision.

Ruth watched her, feeling a queer mixture of inappropriate envy at the very young who are so very sure and sorrow that their certainty was a delusion. Like thousands before them, Karen and Danel simply hoped to live happily ever after. Yet, without that delusion, who would marry at all?

The conversation took place in early October. Louise and Tom were told and had done nothing but try to adjust to the idea since. They did not want an ex-zookeeper as a son-in-law even if he did have an angelic face. Louise's plan for her daughter was graduate school as soon as she finished in May. Until Danel showed up that was Karen's plan also. Graduate school wouldn't appeal to her now, nor to Danel. If he didn't want the first degree he wouldn't be interested in a second one.

Ruth leans back in her chair, taking comfort in the familiar creak of its hinges, and stares at the blank cement wall. Up against it! Everybody to the wall! Man the barricades! Here comes the family with Grandmother behind them all shouting, Wait for me, you rabble! Karen Baby, they do not like it—you setting out on the great highway of life in a milk truck! The great highway of life—straight out of a revivalist's sermon, but not based on demands of a consumer culture for more highways as Karen would think. No. The old Georgia preacher's metaphor was based in the past, on handed-down memories of mountaineers whose great-grandparents had heard of the king's highway. They are almost gone, those people with their ancient English memories. Her own family is an anachronism, one she fights and loves. Her father still hunts in the fall, is proud of his bird dog, his horse, his farm, his position. His construction company is Building a New South, a favorite phrase of his, but his heart belongs to the Old South. The phrase is a thin coat of enamel laid over cast iron ideas about the privileges of whites and the place of all those he calls colored folks. He believes his prejudice is hidden; he believes he is being generous because he has trained himself not to say nigger. He is proud of her, though he cannot understand why she wanted a Ph.D. or why any woman of good breeding can let herself become a liberal. They quarrel about politics whenever they meet. Mother ignores these fights. She gives her energies to good cooking and good causes, raising funds for the symphony, raising cain about busing children to integrated schools. Grandmother, ninety now, mutters genealogies to herself and forgets the names of her great-grandchildren.

"Hey, Miss Logan."

Ruth swings around toward the door. Office hours are beginning.

Jack stands by her desk waiting to be invited to sit down. She has watched him go through the familiar transformation from a clean-shaven, earnest freshman to his present shagginess. No doubt his parents blame the university for the beard and beads. They had, however, insisted on his going away to school, leaving them, leaving Ft. Worth. As soon as he left they got divorced.

"Guess what I made during spring break . . . a coffin."

"Oh God!" Her reaction falls neatly halfway between shock and wry acceptance. How unhappy he would be if he couldn't shock someone.

"I brought it to school with me. It's all lined."

"What color?"

"Red. Satin was too expensive. I got some other red shiny stuff. I keep it in the living room of our apartment. Yesterday I was laying in it studying and fell asleep. When I woke up the kids from across the hall were all sitting there staring."

"Too bad you weren't holding a white plastic lily."

"Everybody chipped in and got me a wreath already."

"What does your shrink say about this?"

"Haven't told him yet. He'll probably say it's a death wish, but that's too simple."

She shakes her head. Maybe it is. All she can see is a frantic need for attention, hard to get in a big school. Like a lot of other students, Jack has tried to look eccentric—nearly impossible now. He's gotten lost in the crowd and made himself a coffin.

Ruth glares at a stack of papers and quizzes to be graded, picks them up, and goes home. She lives in a small house near campus in a neighborhood of old houses and monstrous new apartments. Murray is sitting on the steps when she arrives, so there is nothing to do but let him in. The door key is a dead weight in her hand. All afternoon long she's listened to students, to Jack, then to Rick, who wanted to discuss Shakespeare and astrology. He'd read a lot about astrology, a little of Shakespeare. She tried to explain the Elizabethan concept of the universe to him, knowing she was failing to get him to understand why he couldn't include the poet's writings in his private mythology. Diane came in next to announce she could not get a paper written, a form of surface trouble Ruth knew well. Unconsciously Diane fought against all assigned work. Only self-imposed tasks were honorable, especially since she was involved in an intricate quarrel with her parents, who threatened to cut off all funds if she wouldn't give up studying drama. This semester their required course was shorthand, which Diane was bent on failing. Her parents thought they were being practical. All Ruth could see was the creation of another problem, one really more bizarre than Jack's. Since his father was a doctor he'd had every reason to hate Jack's backyard coffin project. Still, he'd let him build it.

Murray takes the key out of her hand and opens the door himself. A bachelor now though he's been married once, he lives in the same neighborhood. They are lovers though not in love, Ruth has decided, while acknowledging to herself that her pride will not allow her to grant anything more. Constantly reassuring everyone else, she overlooks her own need for reassurance. She doesn't know what Murray has decided. He isn't the kind of man who scatters declarations of love around casually. He is there often enough. Too often sometimes—like today when all she wants is a drink and solitude. Evidently sensing this, he says nothing except, "How's the freak show?" She makes a face and he ambles into the kitchen to get them both a drink. Greeting Murray is like patting a large, friendly, but somewhat wary dog, a German shepherd in charge of guarding nothing but himself—well, no, not a German shepherd. She doesn't like them.

"Murray, what kind of dog would you be if you could be one?"

"I wouldn't want to be one. All I want to be is what I am." He settles in an armchair after handing her a drink.

Since she's listened to people talk about who they are all afternoon she is in no mood to ask for a definition. Though curious about his ex-wife and children, she will not question him about them. Perhaps he is still in love with his wife—if not in love, at least still emotionally bound to her. Strange that we keep halves of ourselves secret from each other; the sides of our lives everyone else knows, we don't. Only my family doesn't know about him. His doesn't know about me. All our friends do. Karen does. She treats him like a father. Is that what we are to her? Idealized, substitute parents. Is that what we are to all our students? We are shadows, though, and they are real. We sit at our desks, Murray in the government department, me in the Bottom, talking, listening. We are hidden away like oracles, me in my cave, Murray in his. We should have enormous ears drawn on our doors. She suggests this to him.

"You listen too much, Ruth. They know you will listen, so they come to you."

"Somebody has to."

"Send them to the counseling service."

"I do, the worst ones, the suicidal, those on dope, excluding marijuana—"

"The divorce cases. That's what I get. They all seem to know I'm divorced. Sometimes I think I should have been a lawyer." He grins, trying to cover his discomfort, but Ruth sees his parted lips as a slash revealing pain. Right now she cannot bear any more misery, not Murray's, not even her own. She would like to be insensate, a stone instead of an exposed nerve quivering in the wind of every passing emotion.

Murray's moustache rests on the rim of his glass. His chair is nearby. She would like for him just to be there, quiet, waiting while the worst, down part of the day is over, waiting till whiskey lulls and she can listen again. But he cannot wait. Though he speaks of Karen, she hears his voice insisting, Me too! Me too!

"She and Danel went down to the courthouse today. They were thinking of getting married there, but it's grubby. I told her they ought to go home to pacify her parents. She insists on marrying here where her friends are. So, she wondered if I thought you'd mind if they got married at your house."

"Here!"

Murray smiles wickedly as though her shock pleases him.

"You are a dog!" Ruth glances wildly at piles of papers, records, books, a pair of Murray's sandals, two suitcases she's never gotten completely unpacked, a series of enormous paintings she is storing for a friend, a week's supply of dirty coffee cups, glasses, and ashtrays. Stranded on one side of the room where its cord had broken is a vacuum cleaner. Above it an old deer head, one her father shot on his first trip to Texas ten years ago, stares complacently. Her disorder she creates and lives within happily. Once a month a maid comes in to make paths around everything; the house is never actually clean. She won't take time to arrange her belongings. At home she camps out. Her office is conspicuously orderly; a wall of books filed according to the library cataloging system, a desk, practically bare because she does her grading at home, two chairs, a few pictures. That is all. Too bad it is so small—she could throw a party there without doing anything more than moving a pencil holder off her desk.

Murray moves his hands through the air as though he is sweeping all objects and objections aside. "You could do it. What she's really asking for is your approval. You know, I believe if they don't get married Karen will spend the rest of her life in libraries. That's what she's been raised to do."

"She's too young to know what she wants. Other than that I have nothing against her getting married. I didn't raise her and I don't think she should wall herself up in the library for a lifetime."

"What are you getting so upset about? I didn't say she was your daughter. She did choose to come to this particular college though. She could have gone to Radcliffe, Wellesley—"

"She wanted to come out west."

"She wanted to come to your school, to be where you are."

"I have never tried to influence her."

"You didn't have to. All you had to do was to be here."

Anger coils within her, cold and perfectly contained. He has put a fatal seal on her, the would-be mother, a woman with no children of her own who must clutch at her sister's child as well as care for every stray that crosses her path. Picking up her glass, Ruth wipes away a ring of water on the table, a futile gesture, for circles within circles mar the wooden surface already.

In her mind flashes a vision of Danel and Karen skipping and hopping through the room toward an impeccably robed minister at the far end. Behind them march the family tree, Grandmother at the top, her mother and father, Tom and Louise, Aunt Judith, all the uncles, their wives, and children spreading out behind them through the yard to the sidewalk, to the street where Danel's white milk truck, washed and garlanded with flowers, stands waiting. And, afterward, Danel's and Karen's friends dressed in motley on one side of the room, her family in drab conventional clothes on the other, glowering at her in the middle, Ruth the Rebel, witless leader of yet another revolution. Mother Courage dragging her children on. Is that what he's saying to me? Oh, it is nothing new, nothing new at all. What childless woman teacher hasn't been called the same? Can't I love anyone without being accused of wishing they were mine? This protected man, so willing to brand others, what is he to me? Where will he be while the wedding is going on? She looks at his sandals and he, following her eyes, promises her he will remove all evidence of their relationship, another word she hates for it appears to her they have none. They are in no way related. Because they are not, she would like to cling to him. An old blues tune drifts through her head. Don't take your shoes out from under my bed. Oh don't . . . don't take yourself away and leave me here alone with them all. I'm so tired—She wants to beg, but cannot. The day is old and she will have to live with herself a long time. He believes—she is sure of this—he is being thoughtful. He does not know that by offering to take his possessions he takes himself away from her. By insisting on secrecy, acting only as a friend of the bride's, avoiding embarrassing questions her family is sure to ask—pokers as well as pouncers, they've never stepped around obvious questions—he avoids standing beside her declaring anything. Rebels attract him, yes; but not enough. He will not dare enough.

"Murray, you might as well take everything, your shoes, your whiskey. There's damned little, isn't there?"

He shoves three empty glasses over and puts his down. "I know you're tired, but just because you've got a wedding on your hands—I thought you liked things the way they are."

"Maybe I did."

He comes across the room to her, and in this apparently unguarded movement she is aware he approaches her with premeditated casualness. He is certain once he puts his hands on her he can change her mind. For half a moment she admires his way with women; the next half she watches him with the detached frozen glance of a victim who has decided on escape at any cost. Going quickly around the table she avoids him and walks into the kitchen. He's left the cabinet door open. All she has to do is reach for his Scotch, one more thing they don't have in common. She drinks only bourbon. On the way back she picks up his sandals.

"Here. This is everything of yours that's in the house."

He takes the shoes and the whiskey. "I don't know what you want. Marriage?"

"For God's sake, Murray! Do you think I'd put you in that kind of box! A double wedding! How sweet!" Her voice shakes with compressed rage. He thought her capable of any kind of duplicity. His retreat to the role of a cornered male, the assumption she is pursuing him, drives her straight past him to the door. "I'm not sure what I want either except I want you to leave. Now."

"I'll check on you tomorrow."

"Don't!" She bangs the door shut behind him, locks it with a furious shove against the bolt, slides her back down the wooden panel, and lands on the floor, legs straight out. As if investigating her body for signs of struggle, she looks down and discovers a run in her left stocking. Has it been there all day? Murray hadn't put up much of a fight. Perhaps that's his trouble, perhaps he never does. Or has he fought so often he's worn out? I will never know. He has no real need of me. Easy. How terribly easy for him to find another woman to sleep with, to drink with. Not so easy for me to find another man. Back to the nunnery. Why did I chase him out? Nothing held us together, no promise, no bond, little love. We were comfortable. We kept each other warm. Murray, my stuffed animal propped on my bed, and I—I was his talking doll, Chatty Ruthie. Pull the string and she says, Hello, have a drink. Pull the string again and she spreads her legs. God! What a mess!

She kicks her shoes off and draws her legs up under her chin. Here I am again and it's not the first time I've been here. All my life I've worked to be independent and what do I get, freedom to show a man to the door and sit on the floor with ladders in my stockings. I've chosen not to lean on men or marriage . . . so what happens? I get leaned on. Before Murray, there was Robert, always ill and me the whole damned Red Cross for him. Before Robert, Tom, who only wanted a legal breeder who'd mind well. Before Tom, Marshall hating his mother for treating him like a baby and me for trying to treat him like an adult. Four lovers in twelve years and God knows how many students. I'd better not count. I could bawl, but I won't. I will fix myself another drink, get something out of the refrigerator to eat, and call Karen. She and Danel will help me straighten up this blasted house and I will give her any kind of wedding she wants here. She can have all the guitar players in town, a bouquet of sunflowers, a whole-wheat wedding cake, fresh orange juice punch. We'll throw brown rice at the bride. I'll wear a dress made of an envious shade of green and play the rueful maiden aunt. Rueful Ruth. When it's over, when school's out . . . I won't teach this summer. I'll go somewhere, to India in monsoon season and let the rain cry for me. No. Self-pity will only get you wet. Better to choose an arid desert hermitage, a mesa somewhere in the southwest where I can build a lean-to for one. She pushes herself partway up, hunkers back as she's seen western men do, and sits dreaming of distant vast skies and windy open spaces.

GTT

So it has come to this. What did I expect? That's what happens to old people in the last stage of life. I'd seen it in other families, a dozen anguished documentaries, known that house of the dead, euphemistically called a nursing home, was waiting for her—for me.

"Go up front and look for Mother. See if she recognizes you." Trial by recognition—Aunt Lucy's idea of how I should meet my eighty-one-year-old grandmother. I live in Texas and have not seen her for three years. Outside it is springtime, May in Tennessee; purple and yellow iris bloom by the wall. Inside it could have been winter anywhere, warm and dark; naked light bulbs dangling from high ceilings disperse the light before it can reach human level. I repeat to myself a promise made before coming, "I will not be morbid."

I found her seated with a cluster of old ladies around a TV set. Grandmother Moore was not looking at the picture. She was staring into space, either a limitless void or some memory of her long past. I hoped she was seeing her private show, a brilliant colored reel unwinding. She had married at sixteen, beneath her—she never said so, but her obsession with respectability proved it. She was from an old Virginia family and he was a mule trader, brother to a moonshiner, nephew to a convict. Her achievement can be measured by the fact that I never knew of the existence of my grandfather's relatives until I was thirty. Aunt Lucy's husband, mellowed by the strain of his own life, told me about "the other Moores" in a bourbon-flavored moment.

She settled the mule trader down on a farm, had three children, and was widowed at forty by a train, an electric trolley running back and forth from Nashville, the nearest city. The tracks bordered some of my grandfather's farmland and he often rode the trolley home from the fields to his front gate. Mr. Moore—she always called him that, never your grandfather, but my husband, Mr. Moore—was lying on the train tracks. Did he get a foot stuck? Was he drunk? Did he commit suicide? No one seemed to know. I was three at the time and believed what they told me: he was waiting for the trolley and got run over. Grandmother moved to town for good. She'd always hated the farm and even before Mr. Moore died she'd had a house in town. She lived on the mule trader's canny investments. Hayfever sent her sneezing out of the state every fall. She went by train and she never went to the same place twice. She did not venture abroad. Her only son, George, lived with her after his first marriage until his second. It was a long time between. Once she wanted to marry again, a man she'd met on her travels. He sent her a dozen red roses and a box of chocolate-covered cherries every birthday. I ate the candy, smelled the roses, and sighed with my grandmother over romantic impossibilities. George disliked the man, a fortune hunter he said. Grandmother said he was a gentleman.

I stood in the midst of the semicircle of women before she saw me. "Marianne," she smiled. "I knew you'd come."

I bent to kiss her. I could have picked her up by myself and carried her out of there. Three years before she'd stood in front of me stiffly wrapped in her corset and fully dressed commanding, "Look!" Then, as if preparing me for some sort of secret religious rite, she'd lifted her arms slowly above her head and bent double to touch the toes of her bright red shoes. Red was her favorite color, but only as an accessory. She wore red shoes or red hats, never red dresses. Mr. Moore's black cane and a black pocketbook are her accessories now. The pocketbook, Lucy had already told me, had nothing in it, not even a handkerchief.

"Did she recognize you?" My aunt flutters like a giant gray moth behind me. Her shades are pale, her hair wispy, her nerves thin filaments on top of her skin. I am very careful with her. I nod yes and tell Grandmother I want to take her for a ride, not knowing what I want except to get her out of the dark place.

The other old women sit mesmerized by the television show while we help Grandmother to her feet. I feel the bone of her arm under the soft folds of unresisting flesh in my hand. On the way out we stop for a moment in her room. There is no privacy; every room is shared. I am introduced to a Mrs. Overton, an old lady in a white cotton nightgown sitting up in bed on the far side of the room. Mrs. Overton starts a monologue about various members of her family who haven't been to see her lately. I light a cigarette and look around wildly for an ashtray.

"They don't give you anything here," says Grandmother. "Look in that cabinet. There's a bedpan you can use."

I find the bedpan and put it on the floor beside my chair.

"Every morning the doctor looks in here and says, 'How are my lovely girls?' The next time he does it I'm going to throw that bedpan at him."

"Now, Mother," Aunt Lucy restrains a sigh. The threat is evidently an old one. She is looking for a sweater. The bureau is rickety and seems about to topple over on her every time she pulls out a drawer.

"I've got nineteen great-grandchildren. Oldest one is thirty-five." Mrs. Overton talks in the direction of Aunt Lucy's back.

I turn toward her slightly, trying to give her some attention. "That's a lot of great-grandchildren."

Mrs. Overton does not bother to agree with the obvious. As I lean down to flick ashes into gleaming white porcelain, Grandmother whispers, "Don't ever let them put you in a place like this."

There is no time for me to answer. Aunt Lucy has found the sweater she was searching for and is draping it around Grandmother's shoulders. Neither one of us suggests she should leave her pocketbook behind, though Lucy has managed to wedge a handkerchief through the handle. Mrs. Overton begins naming her great-grandchildren and their parents as we start out of the room, and in the hall I can still hear her reciting the names of generations like someone permanently stuck in Genesis's begats.

Though the place is generally clean, wallpaper is peeling in a giant swag from the hall ceiling, and the window by my grandmother's bed is so filthy I doubt she can see through it. Over everything—the photographs of children, vases of wilting peonies, fly swatters with plastic flowers attached, and the rest of the useless gilded trash relatives had chosen as gifts—hanging in the air of every room is the unappreciated yet practical suggestion, *You have lived too long. Bless the living by dying.*

We creep out through the sunroom with Grandmother's cane tapping a path before us, a nurse on one side, Aunt Lucy on the other. I follow, keeping my eyes on the car waiting immediately outside the door at the far end of the room.

"Just think, Mother, if you were in a wheelchair, you could zip right along here!" says Lucy too cheerfully in the same voice I use when trying to get my children to eat their vegetables. Grandmother would have to be confined to one soon; she is barely able to shift one foot in front of the other and the cane wavers badly.

"Lucy, I've always told you, you have to use your muscles or you won't have any to use." Her opinions on physical fitness are well known to us all: if you can touch your toes without bending your knees you're in good shape, and sleeping on a hard floor is better for you than a soft bed. In the years between sixty and seventy she'd slept on the floor beside her bed more often than in it. She'd fall asleep in bed, then sometime later in the night get out of it and lie down on the rug with a sheet and pillow. In the mornings after my rare overnight visits her bed would be made up before I saw it. She didn't need witnesses to her stoicism—I doubt she would have called it that—sleeping on the floor was good because she slept better there.

"Now, Mrs. Moore, if you'll just be careful about the doorsill," the nurse warns.

Grandmother cranes her neck and looks up at me, "A pack of old fools!" She steps over the doorsill with a lot of unwanted help, then sinks into the front seat of the car I rented at the airport last night.

Aunt Lucy tucks herself in the back seat and I start the motor. "Where do you want to go?"

"What does it matter?" Her voice is petulant. "I've lived in this town all my life. There's no use wasting gasoline driving me around. You go where you want to go."

There is no place I want to go. The only reason I'd ever come to the town was to go to my grandmother's house. I drive down Main Street, which hasn't changed much since my childhood. All the buildings are small and so wedged together it seems any one of them might pop out into the street propelled by the others' anxiety to continue facing the short thoroughfare. I drive slowly, but even then most of the fronts blur. The only difference I notice is that the liquor store's switched sides of the street.

I remind Grandmother, "When I was a child walking with you down this street I stared in all the windows, but when we got near that store you'd twitch my hand and tell me, 'Ladies don't look in whiskey shop windows.'"

"I know it! Now the whiskey shop's in the building I own." She kept looking straight ahead.

Now I walk into a liquor store and buy a month's supply of whiskey when my husband's too busy to go. The man behind the counter calls me by name and takes my check without asking to see my driver's license. I've looked in and been in liquor stores all over the world, from those that let you sample their wares in Mexico to English wine shops where the vintage year is a matter of great importance. I take a good long look at the window. There is nothing in it but a row of bourbon bottles and a plastic crow dressed up in an evening suit, but that forbidden territory of childhood is still invested with the allure of the sinful, mysterious, and unladylike qualities Grandmother had given it.

"Oh look! There's May Morgan going down the street with a sack of groceries." Aunt Lucy struggles to roll the window down.

"Don't be silly! She's been in her grave for a week!"

"Mother, I tell you it's May Morgan. Look, there she is walking along carrying a sack of groceries." Aunt Lucy succeeded in getting the window down and was flapping her hand. She speaks to everybody. If she acknowledges others they will greet her. Every hello strengthens her existence.

The lady with the groceries conforms to the code by giving her a lavish smile.

"Lucy, she's been buried a week now." Grandmother refuses to turn her head.

"One of you is seeing a ghost," I suggest. They both hush.

We turn up one of the side streets leading to Grandmother's house, a reflex action I realize when I feel Aunt Lucy tensing behind me. Of Grandmother's children she and Uncle George are the only ones left. They both wanted to take their mother home with them, and both were unable to. George's health had been broken by a terrible automobile accident. Aunt Lucy would have to spend the rest of the day in bed, her guilt smothered by tranquilizers, after a visit to the nursing home. Uncle Phillip, well aware of her frailty, could not let her bring Grandmother to their house. Though they had tried they could not find anyone to stay with her at her own house. They dragged in one woman after another, women old enough to be companions, young enough to do the cooking and a little housework, and hopeless enough to have no other means of livelihood. Grandmother complained about each one. None of them were, to her mind, genteel enough. Gentility, that all-enveloping nebulous characteristic admired by her and other ladies of her age, could not be bought. A hired companion was condemned by her wages.

When she was seventy-nine she suffered a cerebral hemorrhage and had to be taken to the nursing home. Ever since she'd left she'd been plotting to get back to her own home again.

We pass the house, an ornate white frame with curlicues of woodwork embroidering the front and side porches and more gingerbread work dripping from the second-story eaves. Grandfather Moore hung a sign on his gate, "Trade In Your Old Mules For New," and settled down on the farm, but Grandmother hated farms then as much as she hated nursing homes now. This was her town house and there was room for the whole family in it, even the second and third generations. I lived here with my mother during part of World War II, and have spent more days than I can remember swinging on the front porch swing.

"The house looks good," I said.

"I spent a good deal of money getting it painted this year. There are renters in it now. They're not what I would call genteel!" Grandmother lapsed into an alarming silence.

Aunt Lucy sighs quietly and I know the battle has been temporarily suspended in my honor. I pull into a driveway across the street to turn around and see that the house which had once stood there on a half-acre lot is gone. Nothing remains but some doorsteps surrounded by trees.

"What happened to Mrs. Laurel's—"

"She passed away." Aunt Lucy has never, in my presence, said that anyone died.

"And after she did they tore her house down," says Grandmother in a raddled voice.

"Mother, Mrs. Laurel's house burned down. Don't you remember?"

Grandmother didn't turn her head to answer. "Anyway, it's gone!"

I don't know of any other place to go and want to do something cheerful so I suggest driving out to my street. I've never thought Marianne St. was a very good name for a street, but Uncle George, who was a real estate man before he drove into his own stone gatepost and smashed himself up, developed the area and named the street after me. We drive through the older neighborhoods out to the edge of town and find Marianne St. I've always secretly wished it could have at least been Marianne Ave., but it is St., and it is suburbia and rather poor at that.

"Nice little houses," Aunt Lucy offers.

"They keep their lawns well," I say, trying to say as little as possible.

"Tacky!" Grandmother pronounces.

Leaving Marianne St., which is mercifully short, I start back to town again. We go around the square where Uncle George still keeps an office on the side opposite the courthouse. He handles a little real estate and the few letters I receive from him are written on his business stationery. He keeps the office, I think, mainly because it's his place to go. Every day his wife takes him to it at ten and picks him up at noon. He goes home for lunch and a nap; then she drives him back to the office at three. Like his father he admires slogans. On top of a file sits a stuffed owl, and underneath the owl on the square wooden base there's a sign which says, "Be Wise, Buy Moore." Uncle George and the owl sit together in the office glaring at the huge granite obelisk in the middle of the square. A memorial to the Confederate dead, it's bigger and even more permanent than his gatepost.

"There's the statue to the Confederacy. Isn't it lovely?" said Aunt Lucy.

I don't know why she had to say that. We had all been seeing it all our lives and no one could have thought it was lovely.

"It's in the way!" says Grandmother, who couldn't possibly have been thinking about civil rights. She meant it was in the middle of the street as it had always been. Contrary to myths about old Southern ladies, she never wasted any grief crying over the lost cause. Gentility interested her; history didn't.

We return to the nursing home and ease her back into her half of the room. Fearing Mrs. Overton will start talking again, none of us look in her direction though I see, with a shifty glance, she's sitting up in bed as still as carved white marble. I sit down beside Grandmother and Aunt Lucy goes to the closet to inspect clothes. Now and then she holds up a dress and shakes her head over a spot.

"How are your children?"

"All right."

"Tell them about me." Her eyes wander toward her bed, but she resists. She tries to sit up straighter in the chair. "What will you tell them?"

I wait awhile before answering, trying to think what would please her best. The facts I know about her life seem meager, and, to her, probably disappointing.

"I will tell them about your house in town with a front porch swing. Those hardly exist anymore."

"Neither do I."

I want to cry, to say yes, you do, to throw out all the junk, and tear the draggling paper off the walls, but I only say goodbye, and take

Aunt Lucy home.

All the way to the house she weeps into an embroidered linen handkerchief and I feel a momentary sympathy for Uncle Phillip. I was born into the family; he has had to spend all of his life adjusting to the Moores. I attempt to comfort Aunt Lucy though I am incapable of giving her anything other than an audience to grieve before. I love her, but her trembling is as great as my anger. We are both too prone to excessive emotions.

After leaving her stretched on her bed, I drive back to Uncle George's office. Crippled as he is, he's the only head of the family. He looks startled when I come in. I have been there only twice in my life, once when I was a child and thought I'd make him a surprise visit downtown. He sent me home. The other time was for the reading of my mother's will. She was killed in a plane crash when I was eighteen. Her lawyer, a friend of George's, decided we should meet in my uncle's office, possibly to make it easier on me—the familiar-place idea. It wasn't familiar, and nothing from that day on was easy between me and Uncle George. He had been named as my guardian until I was twenty-one. My father was killed in the war. He'd left everything to Mother, and she, in turn, left it all to me.

I had one wish then, to leave, to go as far away as possible. Uncle George allowed me to go eighteen miles away to Nashville to college. I told my husband when he asked me to marry him I certainly would if he planned to take me back with him to Texas. He laughed and promised to take me as far away as I wanted to go. To him, my family was archetypal Southern in an interesting state of decay. To me, they were everything I wanted to escape; I longed to be uprooted, to be torn from Uncle George's domination, Aunt Lucy's clinging, my grandmother's determination to mold one more lady. Some people marry into families—I married out of mine. Now I have my own family, and to them their Tennessee relatives are vague people who send them Christmas gifts.

Uncle George asks me about the children.

"They're fine."

"When are you going to bring them to see me? I sure would like to see them before they grow up."

He is a benign-looking old man with thick white hair. His body, so tough once, is cradled in his chair, his arms rest on the chair's arms. A desk, almost bare, is between us, and the owl stares at me from the top of the file cabinet. The feathers are dusty; the glass eyes are eternally bright.

"Will Grandmother ever be able to go home?"

"No. She's in a bad state, honey, and we can't get anybody to live with her. It's impossible these days. Anyway, she runs them all off."

"I know." I smile, trying to be tactful. "The place where she is . . . it's depressing."

"It's the best in town. People are waiting in line to get in there."

When he says this I see a line of wheelchairs full of old people, and behind every chair stands a younger person with a positive smile on his face. My reflections make me shudder in the middle of a warm day. The past, my present grief, my children with their lives before them, morbid ideas about my own old age, have all coalesced in one moment.

I will take her home with me, I decide, take her back to Texas. I could give her a more pleasant place to die. But where in my house, in my life, is there room for the dying? All the reasons for not doing what I feel I should do rush by and fall in a muddled heap in my mind. Our house is small, the children need constant attention, Grandmother needs twenty-four-hour vigilance. I do not have the strength required to meet all those needs.

My stay is short. Before I leave I go to see her for the last time. The photographs of Mr. Moore, my mother, Uncle George, Aunt Lucy and Uncle Phillip, their one child and his children, and the one of me and my children, all on top of the bureau smile like conspirators at each other. It was as though Grandmother wasn't sitting beside me, but Sorrow herself was on the edge of the bed holding a cane. I thought she was indomitable, but she wasn't. She was old, tired, and a little mad.

"Tell the children . . ." She stops because she cannot remember their names. Four or five times in the last week she has called me by my mother's. I wasn't even sure whether she was speaking of her children or mine, but I know what I will tell mine. Your Grandmother Moore boarded the train every fall and went to thirty-eight states, including Texas, at a time when people still counted the states they'd been to. When asked if she ever returned to one of them she usually answered, "No! Why go back to the same old place!" She did not approve of a lady drinking anything more than a glass of sherry, and one glass only, to be "sociable." Her trick for remembering names was to imagine those easily forgotten ones perched on top of her dresser, but toward the end of her life she forgot nearly all. She loved any kind of party, especially card parties, and she had no interest in history, particularly family history. She hated the country, and she lived in town until the day she died.

I left. For a week I'd been living with the Moores again and I'd almost quit thinking; I reacted. The old instincts rose—fear, rebellion, rage, and the overwhelming desire to escape. People on the run used to leave Tennessee in such a hurry all the notice they gave their neighbors was GTT scratched on the doorstep. I left my notice on Aunt Lucy's bed: Gone To Texas. Love, Marianne. So I ran, clutching my guilt to my heart.

The Vulture Descending
Each Day

It was usually quiet at the museum on Saturdays when Mr. Issacs was there. An obscure place even in Austin, a small city where there were few obscurities, it was seldom visited. Located in a block of parkland, well back from the streets, surrounded by straggling cedar trees and high bushes, protected in front by a low rock wall, the Elizabet Ney welcomed the general public with an open gate and a path leading to the front door, but the general public, Mr. Issacs had observed, did not often come to see what Miss Ney had left them.

Saturday was Mr. Issacs's day to serve as the museum's keeper. All week long he looked forward to the one day he would be impeccably dressed in his only black suit with his gold watch chain stretched opulently across his vest instead of crumpled in his side pocket. He walked to the museum, a small, neat man doing his civic duty in his funeral clothes. He thought of his part-time job as a favor he could do the city although he took the dollar per hour pay they gave him. At the end of each month he donated his salary to the upkeep of the museum. It was not an outright bribe. He put the bills in the iron box in the front hall with the sign *Voluntary Contributions* posted above it; if he wanted he could always donate the thirty-five dollars to some other institution. The city, however, needed someone at the Elizabet Ney on Saturdays, and he needed something to do.

Mr. Issacs settled himself at the small desk behind a glass display case. Directly behind him double wooden doors were shut against March drafts; above the doors the only daylight in the room filtered through a wide north window rapidly being overgrown by a jungle of pot plants on the sill. In one corner the cut-stone fireplace had been boarded up to enclose an electric heater still buzzing and glowing. Though the ceiling was high and the stone walls must have been cold early in the morning, the place was now much too warm. He felt like a wizened plant in a dry greenhouse. Straight across the room in his line of vision was a bust of one of the governors of Texas, a rather grim looking old man. Mr. Issacs preferred to shift his eyes to the pleasant ringleted head of the daughter of another governor. All the Europeans except Miss Ney, who had been German, and her husband, a Scot, were segregated in an adjoining room. Mr. Issacs was encircled by Texas governors, judges, and heroes and oil portraits of Miss Ney and her patrons. He surveyed the room, acknowledging, as he usually did, that if his part-time job did not provide much human companionship, it did give him the company of some distinguished ghosts.

He led, he reflected, a part-time life. He was a part-time sleeper, a part-time cook, a part-time dog walker—a continual mourner. His wife had been dead for two years and his recurrent wishful dream was that she was still alive. Yet, she'd died a miserable death. Cancer ate her up and when she was gone everyone said it was a merciful death. He agreed at the time, knowing it was better for her anguish to die, but he would have given the days he had left to him to hear her voice calling his name, her plaintive voice calling him to come to her room and turn her over.

"Who is the man handcuffed to the rock?"

Mr. Issacs, jolted out of his daydream by the intensity of the question, twisted around in his chair to look at a Mexican boy.

"How did you get in?" He was a small boy with a jagged haircut and old but well-shined shoes. His clothes were as clean and neatly pressed as Mr. Issacs's. Evidently his mother cared how he looked. A smudge of dust on his forehead showed he didn't pay much attention to himself. Probably he'd been running his hands over the sculptures. Some of them were not very well dusted.

"The back door." The boy pointed to the room where the Europeans were collected. "It was open." He walked around to Mr.

Issacs's side and braced himself with one dirty hand against the glass case. Yes, he must have been touching the statues. Good sculpture should arouse the tactile sense, though he did not think Miss Ney's figures often did. Who wanted to pat an old baron's stony head—not the children dragged in by culture-conscious mothers. The only thing that ever interested them was Stephen F. Austin's plaster gun, and the fact that it didn't shoot was always a disappointment to the little machine-age monsters.

"Yes, I remember. I unlocked the door this morning." Mr. Issacs tapped the glass top with his dry fingers. The child had asked him something. What was it? He should answer. Visitors hardly ever asked him anything. When he had first started working he'd followed people around from room to room commenting on Miss Ney and her work, chattering, he soon perceived, mostly to himself. He retired to the desk to sit as mute as the rest of the statues . . . the child had asked about a statue, the man handcuffed to the rock.

"It isn't a statue exactly. It's a cast, a plaster cast taken from a statue of Prometheus, the god who brought fire to men."

"Why is he handcuffed to the rock?"

"He is being punished. Those old Greek gods knew how to punish. Because he gave the fire away Zeus had him chained to a high mountain and—" The child was too young to know anything about mythology. He could not tell him about the vulture descending each day.

"Does it hurt him?" The boy looked at his own skinny arms.

"What is your name?"

"Is he real? Does it hurt him?" He stretched his arms out by his sides.

"Yes, it hurts. He does not complain though."

"Where is the mountain at?"

Mr. Issacs sucked in his lower lip in an effort not to correct him. "What is your name?"

"I am called Ricardo. I am eight. Where is the mountain at?"

"Between the *a* and the *t*," Mr. Issacs snapped, the pedagogue in him overcoming caution. He sighed; another one demanding to be taught. He used to see children like that in his classes. They couldn't be stopped and neither could this one. Why, after all, should he be?

It was a brutal story, no more brutal than many fairy tales though, nor half as vivid as a television murder.

"If you are eight, Ricardo, you are old enough to read. Go to the library and ask for a book about Prometheus. Here. This will tell you all about the museum." He lifted a folder from the top of a large pile and slid it across the case toward the boy.

Ricardo's hand closed over the paper; he crunched it into a ball and stuck it in his pocket. "Where is the library?"

Mr. Issacs opened the drawer to the desk and pulled out a city map. "You are here at the museum. Do you see?"

Ricardo nodded.

"Here is the library down here near the city hall. Can you get down there from here?"

"I can go anywheres on my bicycle."

"Good. Go to the library, then come back and tell me about Prometheus."

"You already know." The boy left Mr. Issacs's side and ran out the front door. The museum keeper waited a moment, then got up and followed him. Ricardo was riding away on a bicycle much too large for him. He had to throw all his weight from one side to another in order to reach the pedals. Mr. Issacs shook his head. The child was determined, but he seemed so wary. Of course, he could have told him about Prometheus, but if he'd told him, he would have forgotten. Perhaps he wasn't even on his way to the library. Children were often intensely interested in something they forgot in five minutes. It was better sometimes to be stingy with knowledge. They used to argue about that, he and Kate. Give, she would say, give all you've got. No, you must withhold something unless you want parrots uttering your own thoughts. It's a long way to the library, miles, and that child has to struggle with his enormous bicycle. I know it, Kate! Don't exaggerate!

"Tim!" he called, turning away from the door. There was no answer. Where was he? He was part of the upkeep Mr. Issacs helped pay for, a Negro man who cleaned and dusted; he'd been maintaining the museum years before Mr. Issacs had started to work there.

"Tim?" His voice wavered, a thin echo preceded him through the hall.

"Up here." Tim's answer rolled down. He seemed to be some-where outside, but there were no repairs needed on the tiny front balcony which, with a storeroom, comprised the second level. Plenty of dusting should be done in the big sculpture-filled rooms down-stairs, by the look of Ricardo's hands.

Mr. Issacs started up the narrow wooden steps. "What are you doing?" They were always shouting, he and Tim, like two small boys delighting in the noise they could make in the vacant rooms.

Tim's muffled voice roared again. "Washing winders. I'm settin' here on this winder sill and I'm about to fall off."

Mr. Issacs sighed. Terrible things were always about to happen to Tim, and they never did. "Which room are you in?" He stood at the top of the stairs. A winding circular fire escape led to a tower room on the third level. He hoped Tim wasn't up there. He didn't like to make the stiff climb, and the anatomical studies stacked on shelves, hands without arms, feet without legs, mortally depressed him.

"I'm in the storeroom, part way in anyways."

Mr. Issacs entered the storeroom. Tim's body filled the window in one corner. As the frames were mounted on hinges allowing both halves to be swung inside like French doors, it was completely un-necessary for anyone to perch on the sill while washing them. Mr. Issacs eyed Tim narrowly, wondering if the simple idea of imminent danger made life more exciting for him. Then he glanced around the room. The entire place had been emptied and cleaned, the walls cov-ered with white burlap, and all the woodwork painted white. "What's going on up here?"

Tim stood up, being careful not to catch his starched white jacket on the sill. He wore the jacket for every job. Mr. Issacs didn't know who had provided it, some former employer maybe. It made him look more like a butler than a janitor, perhaps his reason for wearing it all the time.

"Don't you know? We are having a art gallery in here. I been cleaning all week."

"An art gallery? But we have that downstairs!"

"Yes, sir, but this one's going to be pictures."

"What kind of pictures? Whose pictures?"

"Modren artists are going to send some."

Mr. Issacs sucked in his lip and closed his eyes. It wasn't Tim's destruction of the language he minded; he'd grown accustomed to that. Since he'd decided from the first never to play the officious white boss, he had never attempted to correct him. The thing that outraged him was the thought of contemporary paintings at the Ney Museum. They would clash terribly with the nineteenth-century sculpture, making Miss Ney's work appear more outdated than ever. He shuddered at visions of bright gashes of color across the walls.

"It do seem funny to me," said Tim, "but I guess it will bring more people in."

Mr. Issacs opened his eyes and looked at Tim's comforting face. All his life one Negro servant or another—a maid, a yardman, a janitor—had been telling him things were going to be all right. They knew and he knew things were not going to be anywhere near right . . . still, he appreciated the soothing voices. "I grow old . . . I grow old," he murmured to himself. "I am hardly growing old anymore. I am old."

"Well," Tim shrugged, "so am I."

"This must have taken you all week." Mr. Issacs waved his arm to indicate the room.

"Yes. A whole lot of old junk had to be moved to the cellar. I nearly broke my hip on them stairs."

"Did you do the painting, too? Yes, you did. You've got paint on your glasses. How can you see with them all spattered like that?"

"Used to the spots now." Tim grinned. "The whole world's gone polka dotted."

Mr. Issacs surveyed the room again. "It looks good."

The Negro man touched the wall with his outspread hand. "Yes, it looks so good I hate to think of anybody nailing a nail in it, and I'm probably the very one that'll have to do it." His hand slid off the wall. "Nobody told you?"

Mr. Issacs shook his head. "No reason for anybody on the board to call me and tell me what they're doing. I just work here." He began walking about the room peering out the windows. The original glass, bubbled and wavy, was still in some of them. Through these panes the flowering quince looked like soft pink streaks and the surrounding park, a haze of green, but the new glass showed the trees should have been trimmed in the fall and the grass was patched with brown spots. By the end of the summer the lawn would be brown all over. Decay was not pleasant to see even though he felt at home in the middle of it.

"When are the pictures supposed to arrive?"

"Anytime from today on. The show's not going to be for a month. They need a lot of notice, I guess."

"Yes . . . well." Mr. Issacs pulled out his majestic gold watch. "It's eleven-thirty. I'm going back downstairs and get my lunch."

Harder on the heart going down, they said, than going up . . . Mr. Issacs walked slowly down the stairs. There were no restaurants anywhere near the museum so he brought some sandwiches and a vacuum bottle filled with tea with him in a brown paper sack he saved from his weekly visit to the grocery store. Kate had gone to the store every day. She was always running out of something or deciding, at the last minute, to try a new recipe. He went only once a week. The other old people there bothered him, the widows who continued to go every day to buy one frozen potpie and to begin a conversation with anyone who'd listen. It was cowardly to go to the grocery every day out of sheer loneliness. When he did go, Mrs. Dickens, the widow of a college professor (she never ceased reminding him), was always pecking around the green vegetables, an old hen in search of another rooster.

He leaned over the glass case to get his lunch out of the desk drawer, pushing the pile of folders into a sprawling heap. "Lord God in heaven most high!" He drew out the curse, turning it into a supplication before he was finished. At least once every Saturday he knocked over the folders. Stacking them up again, he wondered what it would have been like to have been married to Elizabet Ney. The picture of her on the front of each folder, taken from a painting done in 1859, showed her standing by the bust she had made of King George V, the last king of Hanover. Part of the king's profile was shown, a brooding mustachioed shadow. Elizabet's left arm rested against the stand holding the figure. She had a long face, a long straight nose, dark eyes, dark curly hair, and a determined expression. In her right hand, against the soft folds of her long dress, she held a curved clay-modeling tool. Born in Germany in 1833, the daughter of a master stonecutter, she became a sculptress. Somehow she made the Art Academy in Munich accept her as a student, a young woman demanding to be taught an art open only to men. While she lived in Europe, she made busts and statues of a lot of famous people: Jacob Grimm, Schopenhauer, Garibaldi, Ludwig II, the mad king of Bavaria. She ended in Texas making statues of state heroes, governors, and friends.

A formidable woman—she cut her hair short, wore trousers to mount her scaffolds, kept her maiden name, and called her husband "my best friend"—one of those nineteenth-century heroines who hammered and chipped until the strictures of convention left her free to hammer and chip. The museum had been her studio and her home. From the outside it resembled a small stone fortress.

Her best friend and husband, Dr. Montgomery, stayed over a hundred miles away at their farm, Liendo Plantation, making various scientific experiments and writing philosophical treatises. They had two sons, one who died young and another who volunteered for the Spanish American War. When the children were little, Miss Ney stayed at home with them, but after the first child died and the second grew older, she built her fortress. There was a lot of conjecture about whether she and Dr. Montgomery were really married or not. They were—it had been proved by some busybody who looked up the certificate—but compared to the quiet life he and Kate had lived together, Elizabet Ney and Edmund Montgomery were a dashing pair. Mr. Issacs thumped down the collected folders. Had he ever done anything dashing?

He'd broken off a branch of his mother's prize flowering peach tree when he was fifteen and carried it like a banner before him to give to a girl. The blossoms had fallen off by the time he was halfway to her house. He had volunteered for World War I, more out of a desire to see France than from patriotic motives, and all he saw was the inside of a hospital. He caught influenza two days after his ship docked at Le Havre. He had followed the regular course of a man's life: married, fathered sons, had a profession, retired, lost his wife. His life had been filled with commonplaces, the usual virtues, the general sins, and there was very little time left for anything unusual to happen to him. Perhaps he should develop some amazing eccentricity? He could wear his coat backwards, throw his garbage over the neighbors' fence, call Mrs. Dickens an old bitch to her face . . . but wearing his coat backwards would be uncomfortable, he liked his neighbors, and Mrs. Dickens was only a lonely old widow. He could dye his white hair blue. That wouldn't hurt anyone. Cake coloring would probably do the job. He would be forgiven for his blue hair because of his age—here comes Mr. Issacs, he's harmless really, an old man with a passion for blue. It would be a nuisance. He'd never wanted to be stared at. Why, at seventy, was he thinking of reverting to adolescence? The mind played tricks. Was his failing? Preposterous! His body would fail him before his mind was gone!

Carrying his sack, Mr. Issacs climbed the stairs once more, passed through the new art gallery, and came out on the balcony. He sat down in a folding chair welcoming the sunlight. The balcony, with its dark red painted floorboards and two enormous green tin stars between the railings, was his favorite part of the museum. Under a live-oak tree in the back Tim was eating his lunch. When he got through he would remove his white jacket and lie down in the sun for a nap. Mr. Issacs would have joined him, but he did not want to take off his own jacket and sprawl on the grass; he might get grass stains on his vest and trousers. He preferred his rooftop view where he could watch the birds rummaging in the branches and smell the strong purple flowers of the mountain laurel below, a funeral smell, a funeral tree. No, it was too weak to hold dead weight. He approved of the Comanche burial; they flung their dead in trees to be picked clean by buzzards . . . better than rotting underground, but who could stand the odor of corruption or the bloody sight of the feast? He shuddered at his morbidity . . . forty years of teaching American history, forty years of trying to form an orderly civilized pattern, and still he fell back to savagery.

A car stopped in front of the gate and a young woman in white slacks and a loud yellow shirt bolted out of it. She opened the back door, pulled a canvas, and came hurrying across the lawn with it in one hand. Looking up she caught him staring down at her from the balcony.

"Hello. Are you open?"

"Closed for lunch." Mr. Issacs poured himself some tea and took a sip.

"Can I leave this here?"

"What is it?"

"A picture for your opening."

Mr. Issacs bit into his sandwich . . . ham. He'd made it himself at seven that morning and five hours later had already forgotten what he'd packed for lunch. He couldn't understand why he brought ham sandwiches. They made him so thirsty. He looked over the railing again. The girl was still waiting.

"The door isn't locked. You can leave it in the hall," he said grudgingly, annoyed at himself for his forgetfulness and the girl for her persistence.

"I'd like to see where it's going to be hung."

"The gallery's up here."

"I'll bring it up then," the girl said cheerfully.

Before he could answer he heard her running up the stairs. He threw the rest of the sandwich back into his sack and drank his tea. The girl popped out on his balcony.

"Oh! How beautiful it is up here. I'm sorry I've never been out before. I'm Melrose Davis." She sat down on the railing facing him.

Mr. Issacs glared at her. Her hair was almost as yellow as her shirt, dyed probably, and her slacks were too tight. He took one furtive downward look at her canvas and recoiled. It was a picture of a flat tire, realistic, enormous, and terribly flat, lying on a highway going from nowhere to nowhere. A useless, purposeless object, it made him feel older and more worn out than he actually was.

"Why this?" He made his voice as colorless as he could.

"I don't know—*épater le bourgeois,* I guess. I wanted to see if I could do that sort of thing."

Mr. Issacs could feel indignation rising like steam inside his head.

He had to let a little of it out. "It's rather depressing."

"Do you think so? One of my teachers thought it was funny, but he thinks all pop art is funny."

"Ah," he breathed, not knowing how to tell her why her picture depressed him or if she cared to know. He led her into the new gallery. Melrose leaned her picture against one wall, then straightened up to give the room a quick professional once-over. "The light's fine, now, but you're going to have to get some supplementary spots for the late afternoon."

"This was Miss Ney's bedroom. It was never intended for a picture gallery. She built the light she needed for her work into the house. You'll see nothing but north windows in the studio rooms downstairs." He continued on down in silence, half listening to Melrose chatter about the importance of indirect lighting, the best-lit museums she'd seen, her desire to see the effects of light on snow in the mountains of Greece or did it ever snow in Greece? Mr. Issacs couldn't remember. They went into the first studio room.

"They're all plaster!"

"Most of them, yes. After all, she was working on commission. You can't expect people to give their marble statues back to the museum."

He left her to confront the Texans. The past, by sheer weight of history, would vindicate him. What was a flat tire on a lonely road— nothing. Retiring to his desk he watched her circling the room. She paused for a moment in front of Dr. Montgomery and said something about his beard. Terribly talkative girl. Kate had been a quiet woman. They had a lot to talk about though, married forty-three years and still had a lot to say to each other . . . both of them sitting in the living room remembering their sons, their students, their summer vacations in Mexico, the year abroad when he had a research grant, their long mutual pasts, and in the end, during the last week of her life, all she said was his name, Theo. He dozed and Melrose, seeing him asleep, tiptoed past him on her way out.

Mr. Issacs did not hear her; he was dreaming of two empty rocking chairs on either side of a fireplace filled with ashes. He entered the room and pushed first one chair then the other so they were rocking gently to and fro. When he quit pushing they both stopped absolutely still. The sight of the stilled chairs frightened him, and he ran from the room. He awoke knowing fresh grief—he did not mourn his wife's death as much as he feared his own.

When he was well awake he looked over the visitors' book. Ricardo had not signed it, but Melrose had printed her name in big letters. Didn't they teach handwriting anymore?

Who are they? Mr. Issacs raised his head like an old hunting dog sniffing the wind. A couple holding hands entered the door, letting their hands drop to their sides as they passed. He had seen the woman before, but not the man. She lived in his neighborhood; he was certain he'd met her out walking with her children. She and the man could have been brother and sister; both of them were young and fair, the tops of their heads streaked lighter by the sun, and they had similar expressions on their faces . . . hunger. No, they were not kin, couldn't be, and the man was not her husband. He had seen the husband going in and out of the house. So, she had a lover. Mr. Issacs was delighted. He'd caught a glimpse of a marvelous secret; he was warmed by the aura enveloping them. Oh, he was a disgusting old man, warming himself at someone else's fire . . . probably take up window-peeping next. What was he to do with himself? Did Kate have a lover? No, she wasn't the sort of woman for that. What is the sort? She was not a sensual woman, but she might have been warmer for someone else. Who? Was he jealous of the dead? He'd never questioned her faithfulness while she was living. Perhaps some other man had made her happier than he had. He couldn't begrudge her that. He had been faithful . . . forty-three years he'd been faithful in body if not in mind. He'd looked at other women but he'd never done a thing . . . kissed them on New Year's politely on the cheek and never even patted a passing fanny. He'd been a ninny, a namby-pamby, a respected member of the faculty.

There was Ricardo again. The smudge of dust was still on his forehead and he'd ripped the edge of one pants leg at the bottom, caught it on his bicycle chain. "What have you got?"

"A picture. See." He held it up to Mr. Issacs's face.

Mr. Issacs frowned. It was a picture of Christ, showing his bleeding heart. A cross was glowing in the middle of the heart. "Why have you brought me this?"

"His insides are showing, like Prometheus."

"Hmm," Mr. Issacs murmured and placed the picture face down in front of him. Did the child love the bloody thing or was it only that insides fascinated him? "You went to the library?"

"Yes, on my bicycle I went. I rode fast. I have never gone there before, but I seen it."

"Saw," Mr. Issacs corrected automatically. "And you found the book?"

"A lady found it for me. She let me hold it, and I sat down there and read. They have chairs and tables."

"Yes. You could have taken the book home with you if you wanted."

"I know," the boy said scornfully. "At home my baby sister tears up books." He picked up the picture and put it in his shirt pocket. "The statue in there. It is not true."

"It is a myth," said Mr. Issacs carefully.

"A vulture came every day and pecked his liver out, and it growed back every day. The statue isn't right. His liver don't show. Why don't they show his liver? They don't show it in the book either, and they don't tell me where the mountain is."

"Not they, she."

"She?"

"The lady who made the statue."

"A lady made that?"

"She made everything in this museum."

"How could she?"

"With a hammer and a mallet, a chisel, some talent, and a lot of time."

"Could I do it?"

"Perhaps, if you had the proper training."

"If I made a statue of Prometheus, I would make it better than a woman. I would not be afraid to show his insides."

"That statue was important to Miss Ney, Ricardo. She always

wanted to do Prometheus. Come, let me show you something she was also interested in." He got up intending to take him into the next room and show him the figure of Ludwig II, but he could hear the voices of the young couple. They were quarreling. He delayed entering and began talking to Ricardo again. He was sure the young woman knew who he was. That was good, to be known when he was so old he hardly believed in his own shadow any longer. He had been recognized; he had to be avoided. Negative recognition was better than none at all. He wished he could tell her she need not avoid him. Her secret was hers to keep, but there was no way he could tell her except to stay where he was and talk loudly enough so they could hear him and leave.

"Look," he indicated a bas-relief of a young boy's head. "See how carefully this has been done. It's cut in hard stone, but see how soft the cheeks and curls seem."

"How old is he?"

"I'm not sure. What do you think?"

Ricardo stared at the child's face. "Five, maybe. He is a baby still."

Mr. Issacs heard the voices in the next room diminish to silence, then footsteps. They had found the back door. He took Ricardo past the statues of Travis and Austin to Ludwig.

"Here is a king who went mad."

"He has a lot of clothes on. Why is he so dressed up?"

Ludwig, arrayed in a richly patterned doublet and flowing cloak, stared over their heads, frozen in his frippery and fine nonchalance.

"He admired the king of France, Louis XIV, and he tried to copy everything he'd done. Louis was extravagant in his dress so Ludwig dressed up also." He looked at the boy, who was gaping at him in astonishment.

"Like Halloween?"

"Somewhat."

"Can I go up there?" Ricardo pointed to a raised platform built into the south corner. A hammock hung from the ceiling above it.

"Yes, but don't try the hammock. It's old and the rope is rottten by now."

"She sleep up here?"

"I'm told she did, but I doubt it."

"This high up I see everything."

"She could have a different view of her sculptures from there. It's important to be able to see from all angles."

Mr. Issacs walked over to the side of the cast of Prometheus and touched the plaster leg, stained and worn smooth where many others had touched it.

"This was not a commissioned piece . . . no one paid her to do it." He stumbled in his explanation not knowing how much the child could understand. "You are looking down on it, but I think she intended for people to look up to him. She cared about the gift of fire Prometheus gave to man. She never intended to show his insides."

"Do you know where the mountain is?" Ricardo started down the stairs. He had not touched the hammock.

"In the Caucasus, I believe." He thought of telling him the mountains were in Asia but did not. All the child wanted was a name; the mountain could be anywhere.

"There is another name for him, for Prometheus. I read it in the book."

"What is it?"

"Forethought, a funny name you think?"

"It didn't help him much, did it?"

"No, he got caught anyway." Ricardo stopped at the bottom of the steps and pointed to the open back door. "A man and a woman are out there. Bra-aa-gh!" He snorted. "They're kissing."

Mr. Issacs suppressed the beginning of a smile. "Some people do that in gardens."

"Why?"

"I don't know why."

"I will go to the library and ask for a book about gardens. Then I will tell you."

"Yes," Mr. Issacs nodded, "look for a book about gardens."

Ricardo leaned over the stair rail and looked down at the figure to his right. "Albert Sidney Johnston, 1803 to 1862. Poor Albert Sidney Johnston, only fifty-nine when he died. The card says he's in the

State Cemetery. He has a flag for a blanket. Why did they wrap him in a flag?"

"He was a Confederate general who was killed on the battleground of Shiloh. That's a Confederate flag draped over him. You'd better get a book on the Civil War. It will interest you more than gardens."

"Was poor Albert Sidney Johnston a hero like Prometheus?"

"Prometheus brought the gift of fire to man and endured the torture of the vulture without complaint until Hercules set him free. That is the myth. Judge for yourself."

"His liver growed back, didn't it?"

"It grew, yes. Every day it grew back, and he provided a new feast for the vulture."

"Albert Sidney Johnston was lucky. He didn't have no vulture."

"A vulture," said Mr. Issacs.

A Horse of Another Color

She sits on the beach watching the waves' calm monotony, letting her mind drift to the receding horizon as though she might, by contemplation, reach the world's rim. On either side of her the grayish sand of the Texas coast spreads for miles. Mustang Island, she has told her children, is named for the horses abandoned by Spanish explorers to roam in wild herds years, oh years ago. Whether this is true or not, she does not care to know. Her mother gave her the mustang story, and she passes it along willingly. She has been trained by her husband, a journalist, to remember certain facts, not the obscure myths she prefers, but the ones he has deemed important: dates wars began and ended, routes of major rivers, main products of each region. Basic facts, he calls them. He is in Georgia visiting his parents, a duty she so despises she's planned a way out this year. She does not despise the state of Georgia, its major rivers, or any of its products. She cannot bear Franklin's family. Every year after she's seen them she returns to Cincinnati feeling like a battered child. There is no way, no way at all, she can ever please the Parrishes. They pick at her. Their barbs are expelled in every direction; a general maliciousness pervades their lives and their only defense is to strike first. She has stopped wondering what accumulation of defeats, despairs, or real instances of evil provoked the Parrishes to raise their own children as little Spartans tough enough to endure every insult. In their midst she is only certain of becoming the central target. Her friends call her Sylvia; her husband and her in-laws call her Sissy.

"Sissy, honey, have you tried that new diet club everyone's talking about?"

"No," she told them, but she had tried it, gone to meetings, confessed her gluttony in public, lost ten pounds, had two bad fights with Franklin, and gotten the ten pounds back. Five feet, seven inches tall, she weighs 160. An albatross of flesh! She can feel it even now where the straps of her bathing suit lash her shoulders. She shifts her eyes from the water to stare almost cross-eyed at one arm. Is it burning? Two fingers mash skin. Pinker than it should be? No, not so far.

Abandoning the sight of her own flesh, she stares once more at the sea. Slowly tankers and barges begin moving; the haze is so thick they are ghost ships and to the men on them all the weathered gray beach houses must be a ghost town. Twin visions of reality, both blurred; only the sea is real, the strongest, the most continual, the most objective force.

Two dogs trot past, a black and white one with an orange-brown mixed-breed chow. They stop to sniff at a piece of wood covered with gooseneck barnacles still vainly opening and closing. Up tilt their noses. They distain the barnacles and resume their run full of dog contempt and curiosity. Three surfers, body-proud and, she easily believes, brainless, strut toward the waves lifting their shark-finned boards. Not much action here. The waves are low. How they must dream of walls of water slamming shores in Hawaii or California. For Texans only the gentle slopes of the Gulf are available.

"Mama! Look! A cowboy!" Edwin, her youngest son, drips salt water over her thighs as he points beyond her. He's quivering with excitement. Sylvia hugs him to her.

"Where?"

"There. Over there."

A small man without a shirt or shoes, wearing only blue jeans, rides toward a straggling semicircle of tethered horses far down the beach. Loping along the water's edge, he becomes a centaur figure, the man and horse almost one; he slouches comfortably in the heavy western saddle, his back almost as brown as the horse's.

"Richard! Richard! Look at the cowboy!" Edwin breaks out of arms and runs into the surf calling to his brother. Richard, two years older, is wrestling with an inflated raft, trying to jump on it before the next wave pitches it forward. Anna, standing beside him, laughs.

Will she tell him the rider is not a real cowboy? No. Anna only knows enough English to work as a maid in the condominium. Sylvia has hired her to help with the children in her free hours. With her almost-forgotten Spanish and Anna's barely functional English, they manage to communicate. Happily the woman isn't a chatterer. Much of what they need to tell each other is intuited, for they speak with the body wisdom of women long used to looking after children. She often talks to the boys in Spanish, however, and to them this new language is a game. They point to objects which Anna names: each child conscientiously repeats, *una libra, el teléfono.* Sylvia, waking from a nap, hears them and vaguely remembers her own first lessons from her parents' maids years back when they came down to Port Aransas from Dallas every summer. Richard's and Edwin's interest in the strange flavor of another language is deeply satisfying, for it is both a repetition of her own past and her present excuse for leaving Franklin alone to wrangle with his parents.

"I want the boys to know something about Texas while they are still young."

"They're too young, only five and seven. What could they remember?"

"Everything. Not the details perhaps, but the atmosphere, the spaces, the contrast." She spread her arms wide and Franklin mocked her with what he assumed was a private smile.

"You still feel closed in by this?" He waved a hand indicating Ohio's low green hills.

"Not so much by this . . . more by Georgia."

"You hate my family, don't you? You hate that part of my life."

"They hate me."

"Ah— They don't. It's only their way."

"I wish they would find a better way, a kinder one."

"They're only teasing. It's a form of attention. You're too sensitive. Try not to take them so seriously."

"I have! For eleven years, eleven summers." A month in hell, one every year.

"Sissy, honey, you are so skinny. Take two biscuits. Butter them while they're hot. You need some meat on those bones."

That was the first year, the lean time. She'd just finished college and was working for a modeling agency in Dallas, a job she took in a moment of defiance. Her father judged it unsuitable for a girl who'd studied drama and literature; her mother pronounced it unladylike. Her own desire to be independent was so great she'd quickly decided she could make a living modeling while looking around for something else. But strutting about in other people's clothes six days a week left her no time to do anything except try to compensate for a shallow existence—hours and hours spent arranging her hair, polishing nails, wastes of days before mirrors concentrating on perfecting each physical imperfection, slathering on makeup, creaming away makeup. Even now she detested the helpful scent of cold cream. On weekend nights she wore her old clothes to plays, to concerts, to art show openings. While other women became rare nightblooms opening only in public light, she remained a scornful wallflower watching. One evening at a concert she happened to sit next to Franklin, who was scribbling heavy black pencil notes all over his program. His newspaper had sent him as a last-minute substitute. Their regular critic Franklin denounced as "A man who's a walking percussion section. Only he prefers the music of ice tinkling in large glasses of bourbon and the thud of his body on the floor." Mistaking his capacity for derision as wit and his attention to facts for learning, she found in him the reflection of her own deepest needs. Within six months he'd carried her off to Georgia to meet his family.

Always hungry, she'd given in to the Parrishes. Their hospitality was a force she did not understand then. Looking back she saw she'd been a personified Strasbourg goose; Franklin held her feet while his parents pushed biscuits, country ham, red-eye gravy, creamed fresh corn, fried okra, and fried chicken down her throat. Mrs. Parrish kept two fire-blackened frying pans on her stove and grease was continually sputtering in them. Oh, it wasn't all their fault. She'd opened her silly mouth. Fifteen pounds later she was back in Dallas

out of a job. Franklin proposed, and slowly she discovered she'd
eaten her way into marriage. No, that wasn't the way it was, but the
way it appeared now. The Parrishes were not monsters, not at first.
They indulged themselves and their guests. Their code of hospitality
required them to lavish visitors with food. It was the only attention
they could give without stinting. She dug her feet into the sand and
hoisted herself up to call the children to lunch. At least they were not
overweight; she'd made sure of that. And here on the coast, where
little cooking had to be done, a five-pound loss had shown up
on the scales this morning, the only time she allowed herself to
weigh.

"Mama, a shell." Richard opened his fist to drop a tiny white and
purple shell in her palm.

She studied its perfect curve, color fading from dark purple to lavender, a fragile skeleton washed ashore, preserved from battering
waves by the Gulf's wide shelf dropping ever so slowly inch by inch to
ocean darkness. Looking at the shell she forgot her own heaviness
and, with the quick ebullience that delighted her children, smiled
and said, "Yes, isn't it beautiful. Save it, Richard."

He placed it gently in his red bucket along with a tangled piece of
sargassum, a crab's claw, and a sand dollar. How like Franklin he
looked, his dark wet hair plastered around his face, so preoccupied
with his treasures he would have lost the raft to incoming waves if
Anna hadn't been there to catch it.

Edwin pulled her hand. "Mama, the cowboy— He's riding the
horse in the water. See?" He ran away from her, pointing down the
beach.

She stared in the direction he was pointing, and forgot to tell him
pointing was rude. The man was riding bareback straight into the
sea. The bay reared, throwing his rider into the water; wheeling
quickly, he turned his back to the horizon and streaked toward the
other horses tied up by a dune. The man rose laughing, flinging his
arm up in a gesture indicating an acceptance of the nature of horses
and the futility of trying to teach one anything.

"Crazy," Anna said derisively. For her it was an all-purpose word.
A can opener that wouldn't work, the boys shouting at each other, a

gull chasing an elusive fish, Sylvia's floppy beach hat—all were crazy. She could show scorn, impatience, or admiration by varying her tone of voice.

"Loco," Richard contributed the one bit of Spanish he'd known before coming.

"Si, loco!" Anna laughed while she shook sand out of towels.

"Mama, I want to ride a horse," Edwin was demanding.

Richard intervened as he often did. "Mama doesn't like horses." Only seven, he knew her better than anyone else in her family.

"Anna?" Edwin pleaded.

"Me? No! You!" She laughed and pointed at him, then shook her head slowly to prove it was impossible. At times like this she seemed almost a child herself, a pretty adolescent child.

"Mama, can't I?"

"Someone will have to go with you."

"You go with me?"

"We'll see." It was hard to deny Edwin.

"That means no," Richard said.

Edwin ran ahead of them, leaping up every few steps. "A cowboy! I will be a cowboy!"

Anna glanced toward Sylvia, then went after him.

"Stop. You fall." She pointed at the dunes rising and sinking on either side of the walk where railroad vines, their lavender flowers wide open earlier, had closed against the noon sun. A breeze riffled the tops of the sea oats.

After lunch Sylvia made Edwin lie down. Richard sat on his bed reading. She fell on her own bed, grateful for air-conditioning; even a sea breeze could not blow away the afternoon sun's heavy stare. As usual, she dreamed, and, as usual, she welcomed the dream, for the most vivid moments of her life were lived in this hour. Out of the darkness she rode into a bright, terribly bright day on the back of a yellow horse. Beside her, on a black horse, rode a man she could not see. They loped easily across a field of wild flowers, bluebonnets, orange Indian paintbrush, yellow and brown Mexican hats which nodded and danced. Hundreds of sweetly smiling old ladies in old-fashioned blue bonnets moved sedately in an outer rim around stiff, strange Indians. Self-absorbed, they scarcely seemed to notice the flagrant Mexican hats' wild bobbing. Anna's face, almost entirely hidden by a sombrero brim, passed close to her and gave her a solemn wink. Oh, look, she called, look at the flowers dancing! Entranced by their movement, she wanted to stay watching for hours, but the other rider caught her horse's bridle and led it away as if she had no will of her own but was entirely subject to his. Stop! We must stop! They were going downhill through a forest. At the bottom flowed a river with sandy banks. The black horse bent his head to drink. Her yellow one, without saddle or bridle, rolled and rolled on the sand. Delighting in his freedom, he plunged toward the deepest part of the stream, where he stood to let water rush over him. She looked around for the man. He had disappeared. The black horse whinnied and came trotting toward her; heavy stirrups inlaid with silver bounced against his side. She stood up to meet him wondering, What will I do now? What's to be done now? Her horse swam to the opposite shore. I must ride across the river and catch my horse. I must, but she could not bring herself to mount the wicked black horse.

She woke feeling a terrible loss, a constriction in her throat as though she'd almost screamed, Come back! What had she wanted? What did she miss? Her throat hurt so with the withheld scream that she ran to the bathroom, turned on both faucets, and tried to let it go. All she was able to make was a muffled gargling noise.

Water swirled through the white porcelain, and Sylvia, dipping both hands into clear nothingness, splashed her face with it, muttering, "*Fantasia!* I was dreaming *Fantasia.*" But, if I'm going to have Disney dreams, better *Fantasia* than one of those full of too cute animals. This is what comes of living with children, taking them to movies. Your own subconscious gets Disney drenched. Those horses — Not from Disneyland. Why did I ride a yellow horse? Yellow-horse. Indian name from something I must have read. The black one . . . threatening. Black, the cliché color of evil. Wickedness. Why did I assign wickedness to a horse? She wiped her face with a scratchy clean white towel, conscientiously ignored the scales, and went back to sit on the edge of her bed. No evidence here of any struggle. Covers pulled back in a neat triangular fold. Who was the man? Franklin?

She tried to raise his image in her mind and found him in his parents' home sitting at the dining room table folding a napkin into a neat rectangle, pressing it with the heel of his hand, a characteristic gesture. Franklin, the elder son, the favored one, gone almost completely gray at forty-two. He would be talking, arguing with his father about something, but speaking gently with heavy courtliness, asserting his superiority by displaying his superior manners. She had told him his contempt was only faintly covered by courtesy. It was like a male model covering his homosexuality with a tough grin, but she had not told him that. The implication—he would have insisted on seeing one—would have stung, and Franklin, raised in a family of warriors, could easily attack with his most obvious weapon. He was aggressively sexual. Oh, the battle of the bedroom! Sylvia got up, ready to run out of hers to the swimming pool. Glancing at her watch, she saw it was 2:30. She'd slept just half an hour. It was too early to wake Edwin. She sank down on the bed again. Yes, the battle. For a week she had put it out of her mind as something she had to quit thinking about for a while, though she was aware her time in Texas was as much a vacation from Franklin as it was from his parents. Their first year had been happy. She had wanted to enjoy herself and she did, had wanted the children and had them. What had changed? When had she grown so passive and Franklin so demanding? She avoiding sleeping with him whenever she could, and he continually accused her of becoming sexless. Would some other man produce the same reaction? Was it only Franklin or was her despair totally self-produced? In one of his most bitter moments he'd dropped his cover of polite insistence and said, "You'd better stay with me. No other man will have you."

Looking down at stretch marks on her belly as she wriggled into her bathing suit, Sylvia wondered if he was right. She ran her hand over the sagging flesh. The marks were in part honorably acquired through two pregnancies. If she had not gotten so overweight would there have been so many? Stuffing herself into her suit, she buttoned the top straps, rubbed lotion on her shoulders, which had been sun-burned after all, and went to wake Edwin for their afternoon swim.

Up close they were tawdry-looking animals, not the magnificent black and yellow horses who galloped through her dreams. She could hear their hooves even now stamping the ground as though they despised it, too proud to stand quietly for one minute. But these poor nags, bones stretching skin, heads bent toward a crooked line of baled straw serving as a fence, were obviously being used up. There were only two she could look at without feeling pity, a big sorrel whose angular shanks made him almost comic and the young bay she'd seen in the waves.

The man, older than he'd appeared on horseback, squinted against the morning sun. He was one of those undernourished, tough, small men who made their living by petty thievery in skimpy games, the essence of every carny type she'd seen. Before he said a word she could readily imagine him shouting, "Step right up, little lady, and try your luck. All you gotta do is knock down these three wooden bottles with four balls and you get your pick of the prizes." She had never truly wanted any of the prizes—fluffy pink bears or cheap glass dishes—but she'd wanted to knock the bottles over.

"They are weighted." Her father rumbled behind her. "Even if you hit them you can't knock all of them over. At least one is extra heavy." She would try, for to pass them by meant giving up a chance of proving her skill as well as denying the real existence of fortune. At the unlucky age of thirteen, she'd had faith in luck.

"Save your money and buy a bear," her father advised, though he should have known better; her bed was already cluttered with stuffed animals.

She tried every time. She had to. She did not like the blaring music, the garish lights, or the oily popcorn smell of the carnival. There was only a desire to knock something over, and when she failed she solaced herself by insisting on riding the bumper cars though her parents tried, unsuccessfully, each time, to steer her toward the babyish merry-go-round.

"How much is it for an hour?" Edwin had pulled away and was

trying to pat the bony sorrel's nose. Richard stood by her.

"Where're you folks staying?"

"Over there." Richard pointed to the condominiums.

She wished he hadn't. If the man knew he would boost his prices. They were expensive new apartments. Sylvia, always careful with the money her parents had left her, had chosen them mainly because they were built on the same part of the island she'd visited as a child. The cottages they'd stayed in had been demolished, yet the landscape remained familiar. Sometimes, it seemed to her, she could almost see Cactus Court's faded pink stucco walls with the maguey by every door and hear her mother's sad voice saying, "Century plants. They bloom only once in a hundred years, then they die." And her father's voice, "Nonsense, Evelyn! You're filling the child's head full of rubbish. It's a maguey, an agave. Damn things bloom all the time." He did not like myths; she and her mother preferred them.

"Five dollars an hour."

Sylvia shook her head, dismissing the memory of a century plant's extravagant bloom, a bouquet of waxy white bells.

"Five dollars. That's all I brought with me. I tell you what, Richard. I'll go with Edwin for half an hour and you can ride for the other half."

"Why does he always get to go first?"

"He's the youngest." She lowered her voice. "He'll have to go with me. You can ride all by yourself when we get back."

"Let me ride with Edwin."

"No. I must do it." She looked at the man, half expecting him to smile at the explanation he must have heard many mothers use. His face remained blank.

"We'll take that one."

Edwin was safely hoisted on the sorrel. The man turned to Sylvia, who was wondering if her jeans would split when she tried to mount. Ignoring him, she swung awkwardly up into the saddle. The horse ambled away slowly. She couldn't bring herself to kick him into a trot. Simply being in the saddle seemed to satisfy Edwin although he wanted the horse to walk near the water's edge.

"He's afraid, isn't he, Mama?"

"Yes. He doesn't like sinking."

A small eddy she hadn't noticed sucked at his hooves. He shied, swerving wildly away from it. Still clinging to the horn, Edwin shouted, "That was fun! Make him do it again."

Sylvia trembled inwardly—her whole heart had lurched following the outward curve of the horse's body—hugged Edwin to her. "No. It's too dangerous." Rous, rous, rous, the little waves whispered. The wind blew steadily, whipping her hair into a mass of tight curls, burning her back. Riding in bluejeans over a bathing suit was uncomfortable; double layers of binding material encased her stomach and thighs. Why had she worried so about looking ridiculous riding in a bathing suit? Everyone did it, and what did it matter that she was fat; there were fatter people exposing their masses of flesh all along the beach. At 10:20 she turned the horse back toward the corral, and he broke into a lumpy trot.

Richard was waving flies away from the other horses' heads with a dirty cotton bandanna. "It's Roy's," he explained, and nodded toward the man bridling the young bay horse.

"Here." Sylvia took the handkerchief and gave him her watch. "Be sure to come back in thirty minutes. We'll wait."

Edwin, apparently losing interest in the novelty of riding, allowed himself to be taken out of the saddle without a murmur. In a few minutes he was busy scooping a hole in the sand. Sylvia sat down on the nearest bale of straw and began flopping the bandanna ineffectively.

"You don't have to do that." Roy, standing somewhere behind her, commented dryly. "It don't do much good anyway."

"Are they your horses?"

"None of them but this one." He jerked his head in the direction of the bay. "Fellow down near Padre has a stable. I bring them out here for him. If they were mine I wouldn't have them on the beach. It's bad for them when the sand blows, gets into their lungs. I only bring mine now and then."

"I saw you riding him yesterday—in the ocean."

"He threw me. Always does." He sat down beside her. "I'm training him to ride down on Padre. After a few miles down there you need four wheel drive, or a horse. Sand's too soft, too changeable for a car."

"Changeable?"

"It shifts. Padre's further out to sea than Mustang. Wind hits it more."

"Couldn't you walk?"

"Some crazy kids with backpacks try it. I want to ride all the way down to Mansfield Channel. That's over sixty miles."

"Why?"

"Why not?"

As she stared at him, she refocused his face in her mind. The lines around his eyes no longer gave him the appearance of a shrewd, small-time con artist. No, there was something here at once more ordinary and more anomalous than she'd seen at first. Eyes dominated a face carved by long resistance to sun and wind; the lines around them were the result of years of squinting against glare. His cheeks were wind-worn flat to high arched bones; his long dark hair was as tangled as her own. All that she could partially understand, but even though she wished to she could not comprehend the enigma of his being or his desire to ride an immense stretch of sand.

In the days to come she wondered about him often. Every morning now she rode with the boys. Roy, who wanted somebody to talk to and apparently did not care whether anyone else wanted to rent a horse or not, went with them. He put Edwin and Richard on two ponies he'd started bringing as soon as he saw they would be regular customers. Sylvia rode the bony sorrel and he rode beside her. They made a curious parade—the large sunburned woman on a lazy nag, a small brown man on a spirited bay, and two little boys straggling nearby on Shetlands. Both of them jumped on and off effortlessly now. They stopped to pick up a shell, to exclaim over the expiring sail of a Portuguese man-of-war, then raced ahead, shouting as they passed their mother.

Unlike many men she'd encountered, Roy seemed to have almost no past, or none he'd talk about. He'd always lived on the Texas coast, preferably on an island. Obviously he had watched all forms of life about him. He showed her the holes ghost crabs burrowed in

the dunes, collected sea beans for the boys and warned them the ker-
nel was poisonous, gave her a snail shell with purplish whorls, and
identified it as a fresh-water one, probably washed to the islands from
a Mexican or Cuban river. If they stopped to walk out on the pier he
could name all kinds of fish Sylvia had never seen before—ribbon
fish, hammerhead shark, leopard ray, hardhead cat, sheepshead.
Richard and Edwin were entranced. One day he brought his collection of glass floats, clear aqua, green, brown, lavender bubbles
wrapped in netting, carefully nested in newspaper. They drifted in
on strong spring currents.

"At home I keep them on a windowsill to catch the light."

Sylvia, noticing his reference to home, wondered where his house
was, but he offered no further explanation. She was drawn to him, to
his loneliness, to his self-sufficiency, yet she thought his life was
appalling. What did a beachcomber do in the winter, huddle by a
driftwood fire and pray for the cold season to pass?

"It's the best time. No crowds then, only the people who live here.
Sometimes I work on a ranch. Toddie Lee Wynn's got a big outfit up
on Matagorda. I don't need much money. There's only me and one
horse to feed."

She was touched by this simplicity. "I envy you."

"Why?" He had a slow, crooked smile.

"Oh, for the usual reasons anyone like me would. You're not
rushed or bothered by a lot of things, places you have to be, people
depending on you. I belong to three carpools, one for Edwin's kin-
dergarten, one for Richard's tumbling lessons, and another for his
judo lessons."

"Judo? For a kid?"

"Yes. We thought he should learn self-protection early. A city—
Sometimes it isn't a safe place for a child."

"I couldn't live in a city."

"No, you wouldn't like it."

"Your husband, does he?"

"He works there. We moved from Dallas to Cincinnati. I mean . . .
we've always lived in a city. It can be pleasant. The symphony's
good." Symphony. That meant nothing to him. How could the for-

mal collection of men and instruments, the disciplined beauty of their music, mean anything to a man whose ears were full of the sounds of waves and bird cries? How could the joy of being anonymous in a crowded square on a windy, cold day, or the pleasure of an hour alone in a museum, be told to him?

"Where would you rather live, here or there?"

Sylvia shifted away from the sand castle they had been helping Edwin build. "That's not my choice."

He stood, brushed the palms of his hands across his seat, then came over so close to her she could feel the heat of his body.

"What if it was?"

"I . . . I don't know." Distracted by his nearness, she leaned away to grasp a handful of wet sand to dribble on the castle's turrets. He remained where he was, so when she swayed back toward the castle, her arm grazed his leg.

He knelt beside her, smelling of horses, salt water, and sun, an agreeable mixture she'd grown used to. "You don't get to do what you want to very often, do you?"

"Not many people do."

Edwin came running out of the surf to sprawl on his towel and admire their castle. Ignoring him, Sylvia went on arguing. "Even you—You don't like bringing the horses down here."

"That's just until I've got my own ready for Padre."

"Why must he be able to swim in the ocean?"

"To cool off. It's a long way down there and no shade except from the dunes."

"Why don't you ride at night?"

"I will some."

"Mama, where are you and Roy going?"

"I'm not going anywhere. Roy's planning to ride down to Padre Island."

"Why?"

"Ask him."

"I always wanted to. That's all. It's something I want to do."

Sylvia got up and began collecting their belongings for the walk back to the apartment. Anna was working on the morning shift this week and could not come till afternoon.

The boys were in bed asleep, the air-conditioning had been turned off. Every window was open. The curtains, even though they'd been pulled back, flapped lumpily. Sylvia knotted the pull cords around them and went out on the small porch to gather up bathing suits before they were carried off by the wind. She took them back inside, distributed the suits on the doorknobs of each bedroom, stopped to straighten a pile of half-read books on an end table, then went back to the kitchen to make coffee. In the last week she noticed she moved more quickly to do everything, whether it was pulling her clothes off hastily to run to the beach or rapidly wheeling a cart down a grocery store aisle. Swimming twice daily, riding every morning, eating simple meals—opposing the children's desires for hamburgers and peanut butter—living without the pressure of Franklin's yearnings for fried chicken—helped her lose weight. Five pounds a week, an astonishing rate to her. Immersed in this routine, she'd quit reading much; her afternoon naps now were short deep sleeps. When she dreamed she couldn't remember anything. She'd thought she would miss her rich fantasy life and was delighted not to. Secondhand experience, all of it, as Franklin had often warned her. Some was needed, but she had been overdosing herself on dreams and on stories of other people's more adventurous lives. Franklin would be pleased. Franklin . . . Oh hell! She would have to call him. That was what all the twitching about was caused by, anything to avoid the moment of confrontation with him.

She poured herself a cup of scalding black coffee, put the call in, and sat down to wait for the phone to ring. Long distance took awhile on the island. With one hand she raked through the snarled curls on her head; no amount of brushing seemed to help.

"Sissy?"

"Yes." She'd forgotten, as she usually did when away from him, the heavy southern accent that covered his voice. Whenever he was in Georgia he spread it on like butter.

"How are the boys?"

"Fine. Very brown. Richard caught a fish and wants to bring it home with him. Edwin's become an expert on sand castles."

"I've missed you-all. It'll be good to see you tomorrow."

"Franklin, that's why I called. We won't be in tomorrow."

"Why not?" Demand hardened the melting syllables.

"The coast is good for us. I've lost ten pounds."

"That's encouraging. Just be sure you don't gain it all back when you come home."

"I'm going to stay two weeks more."

Dead silence.

"Why?"

"Because . . . I want to. I'll lose another ten pounds and come home looking like a sylph."

"Sissy, you can diet anywhere."

"It's easier here."

"But I want you to come home. I've missed you here. I'll miss you even more in Cincinnati."

"You can manage well without me. It won't be long."

"It's already been two weeks."

"I know."

"You don't miss me?"

"I'd be happy to have you here. Everything's simpler. I don't have to run a thousand errands and the boys are quite happy. I have a Mexican girl who helps me with them. They're picking up some Spanish."

"You know I can't run down there. My vacation ends on Monday."

"Yes. Well— I want to stay though."

Once again, like an unseasonable cold wind blowing off Lake Erie, silence howled between them.

"It's your money."

My parents left it to me, not mine because I earned it. That's what he means. Never mind. If I take up that gauntlet, I am lost. Indifference is my only shield.

"Yes. Tell your parents hello."

"I will."

"And, I'll see you two weeks from now."

She put the receiver down and continued to sit running her fingers through her hair. A voice from the porch startled her, a muffled voice calling her name. Running to the windows she saw Roy on the other side of the railing.

"Can I come in?"

"Yes. Sure. You frightened me for a moment."

"How do you get in these places?" He jumped over the railing.

"From the back usually." She followed him into the living room. She'd never seen him inside before. His place was outside, on the beach with the dunes or ocean as a background, a setting that diminished everyone. Out there even she felt smaller. Inside, wouldn't the contrast between them be greater, wouldn't he seem physically smaller and she, larger? No, he looked exactly as he usually did except it was evident he'd shaved lately and his shirt was clean.

He stared at the books scattered around the room, as though he were in alien territory.

"Do you read all these?"

She laughed. "No. I'm halfway through some of them."

"But you will read them all?"

"Maybe. Would you like something to drink? I'm afraid there isn't much here. Just coffee and a bottle of wine."

"Wine, if you'll drink some with me."

"I should stick to black coffee. I'm trying to lose weight."

"Why?"

"I . . . I used to be thin. I like myself better that way."

"You look all right the way you are."

"Thanks, but I don't think so. Neither does my husband." She handed him the wine and a funny kind of corkscrew with two levers on either side. "Will you open it?"

"I would, but I never operated one of these before. The only wine I've ever drunk comes in half-gallon bottles with screwed-on tops."

"Oh. Well, bring it in here." On the other side of the kitchen's bar she reaches for a glass on an upper shelf, turns, and puts it in his outstretched hand.

"I . . . I didn't come here to drink."

"Oh?" She presses down on the levers with both hands and the cork comes out with a short pop.

He takes a glass full of wine from her and, marvelling at his own control, puts it down slowly on the counter.

He and Sylvia are exactly the same height. In the kitchen's bright light he watches her face, notices freckles strewn across the bridge of her nose, her eyes, blue-green, alert, almost fearful. She licks her lower lip, holds it for a moment with her teeth, lets go.

He takes a step toward her and says with childish simplicity, "It's you I want."

"Why?"

"I don't know. I just do. There's no why to it."

"You think I ask too many questions?"

"Sometimes."

Everything about her is soft. He sinks against her as though he has at last found a resting place.

"Wait. The children—" They are lying on the kitchen floor, the ceiling light shining down on them like a tiny sun. Her skirt is rumpled up around her waist. He has one knee between her legs. "My room," she says, rolling over on her side. He follows her out of the harsh light to the darkness.

Sylvia rises the moment Roy shuts the back door. On tiptoe she goes to the window to watch him walk off. The growing distance between her and the receding figure, his shoulders slightly hunched against the chill of early morning, twists her heart. He appears so utterly unprotected she wants to run after him, fling her body between his and the approaching fog, and shout, "Don't go. Stay here with me. I will keep you warm."

Quickly she runs to the children's room to cover them with the blanket they've kicked off during the night. My children, so beautiful sleeping. A gurgle rises from Edwin's red plastic bucket on his side of the bed. She walks around and nearly laughs aloud at the sight of a tiny frog sitting on a rock deep within.

Her joy is so immense she cannot possibly return to an empty bed. Going to the kitchen to make fresh coffee, she watches the sunglow move up from the Gulf to spread over Mustang Island. Red at first, it becomes paler as though it had had no strength at all, its deceptive force hidden in haze which will be burned off by noon.

Roy will be eating now. I will see him again in two hours. I wish he could have stayed. The boys . . . can't involve them in this . . . this. What have I involved myself in? Oh, I'm too happy to care. What does it matter? Franklin. Will I go back to him after? Probably. Must I decide now? Wait. Was he happy, Roy? With me? With himself? With us?

She touches her cheeks, burning with inner heat spreading to every part of her body. Wrapping her arms around her waist, she holds herself in an effort to suppress the immense desire she feels for him. Her longing is so great she could jump over the front railing, run past the swimming pool, over the walkway, and out to the beach, naked except for a frilly nylon robe that would surely come untied as she ran. She laughs aloud. Fat woman in love. He did not mind the disparity of their bodies; he almost seemed to relish it. Could he have a grotesque lust for fat women? No. I'm not a freak, not a circus fat lady. I'm thirty pounds overweight and my imagination runs wild. Why must I discover something bad, why must I punish myself by summoning up the most banal evil? I've done nothing wrong, hurt no one. Why can't I have something I want, something I need, for a short time only? All my life I've done what I was supposed to do. I've been as moral as hell and what has being good gotten me? Two children I adore, yes, but in-laws who don't like me and a husband I don't much like.

She stirred her coffee, a habit which irritated Franklin.

"Why must you continue to move a spoon round and round a cup when there's no sugar or cream to stir?"

"It's a comforting sound. Why are you so annoyed? I don't do it in public, only at home."

"Home is where I happen to be with you most of the time."

Too often when he was looking for someone to attack she was the most available victim. Oh, he would be kind later, polite in his most gentlemanly way, wooing her with penitent phrases. "I don't know why I must make you so unhappy. Forgive me. I want too much I know. You see, I want to be loved in spite of my meanness."

He knew what was wrong with him. Most people did, but Franklin used his self-awareness as an excuse for lack of self-control, which would have been all right if only he allowed anyone else the same indulgence. He would not. Even the children were supposed to live in complete harmony, never giving way to childish rage.

"Franklin, didn't you ever fight with your brothers?"

"If we did, we fought where no one could hear us."

"When you got older maybe. When you were little?"

"I don't remember."

A fox gnawed at Franklin's belly all his childhood, all his life, a little sharp-toothed skinny one, well hidden beneath his shirt. Because of the fox she let him have his way. Richard and Edwin fought in the basement, the backyard, the kitchen, or in their room. She spent a lot of time keeping herself and the children out of his way. There were only two luxuries he allowed himself, frequent bad temper and music. Though music hath charms, the beast within Franklin could not be entirely soothed. As the newspaper's art critic he would have been unhappy if he couldn't find something displeasing about a concert. She sat beside him, forgetting herself and the world utterly, yet before the last bars were finished, she would wince inwardly at the fault-finding diatribe to come. If she disagreed or complained to him about his perfectionism, he flung the banner of ART in her face and began his lecture on aspiration. He was paid, he reminded her, to be a perfectionist. Never was a man more suited to his work.

It was eight before she could get the boys ready to go to the beach. How could she be sure Roy would be there, that he hadn't somehow subtly changed, that he still wanted her? The panic of love, so like magic it might disappear any minute, fumbled her fingers, blinded her. Edwin's shirt was impossible to button. She couldn't find her comb or Richard's snorkel mask. Hurrying to the beach, she felt like an abject fool, but Roy was there, waiting by the end of the boardwalk, with their horses.

"Mama was in a hurry."

Richard the tattletale. She could have hit him.

Roy grinned and took her hand as if to help her. "I was fixing to come get you."

She was so relieved she thought she could easily slide out of the saddle. Instead, she clutched the prickly long hair of the horse's mane with one hand.

They loped down the beach, startling sandpipers into stiff-legged runs and sudden flight.

"Why don't you ride down Padre with me?"

"I couldn't."

"Why not?"

"I'm not that good a rider."

"Yes, you are. Come with me."

"I can't. The boys . . ."

"You could leave them with the Mexican girl."

"Not all day."

"Two days and two nights. She'd do it on a weekend."

"I don't know, Roy."

"Come with me. It's beautiful down there."

Anna spent the night on the apartment's couch so she wouldn't have to get up so early. Sylvia tiptoed into the boys' room and touched them both gently on their foreheads. Out the kitchen window she could see the headlights of Roy's pickup moving through the fog. A trailer carrying both horses was attached. Together they became a queer bisected monster, something just landed on earth stumbling about trying to find its way. Glancing toward Anna, she noticed the serenity of her sleeping face. Last-minute anxieties rushed through her mind. Don't let Edwin get too much sun. Richard needs eardrops after he's been in the pool. Yes, I already told her that. I shouldn't be going. I've never left them, not even for one night. Why am I abandoning my children?

Roy tapped lightly on the back door. "Sylvia?" His voice, low yet urgent, drew her. She must go, she had promised. He caught her as she stepped out into darkness.

"I shouldn't—"

"They'll be all right. You worry too much."

"Yes. I know." She let him reassure her. In a dreamlike trance, as though hypnotized by the sound of his voice, she climbed into the

pickup. Soon all she could see of the condominiums was scattered
guard lights, white holes in the night.

"Sleep."

"Now?"

"Try. It won't be good light for an hour."

She put her head down against his knee and closed her eyes
tightly, a child playing hide-and-seek with the sun. It . . . I'm always
it. After counting to a hundred she sat up again.

"I can't. I'm too excited." For a long time she stared out the window. Gradually blackness lifted to gray. In ponds made by inland
cuts she saw blue herons feeding. Ghostly still, they stood in gray-
blue clumps above dark water, waiting as she waited. A red band
streaked the horizon on Roy's side. How many years had it been
since she'd seen the sun rise?

At Padre a coyote slipped through the low dunes near the park
rangers' station. As Sylvia watched his slinking, sideways gait, a chill
ran over her arms. "I've never seen one outside a zoo."

"The rangers probably feed him. Usually you can't see them in the
daylight. That one's lost his wild."

"Why are we stopping?"

"To sign up. Since I'm taking you with me."

His reasons for doing anything were often stated elliptically. He
was out the door and halfway up the steps before she caught him.

"I don't understand."

"They like to know . . . in case anything happens."

"What could happen?"

"Anything. Nothing. I'm just being careful. I'll tell them where
we're going and when we'll be back. If we don't get back when we're
supposed to, they'll come looking for us."

Looking up at him on the step above her, she realized it was extra-
ordinary for him to tell anyone what he was going to do next. Her
own life was neatly portioned out in yearly stacks divided between
the boys' school dates and the annual holidays. Everything was so
planned, so regimented, she'd almost forgotten she'd had to make
the plans. Roy ambled from one thing to another, pushed only by the
changing seasons and his own wishes. He could, when he wanted to,

envision some sort of future. He'd trained the horses for this trip, made the sorrel walk into oncoming waves, trained her to ride bareback, to fling reins aside and swim for shore the minute she felt the horse panic. In the back of the pickup, protected by an old tarp, were saddle bags of supplies, canteens of water, food, bedrolls. They would be self-sufficient; he preferred this above all else. Stopping to sign in at the ranger station was necessary only because she had agreed to go. For this willingness to reveal his plans, she was grateful.

They left the pickup and trailer parked where the blacktop road ran out at Malaquite Beach. The long straight line of a concrete government building, slatted walkways open, bathhouse and restaurant grouped in square towers, dominated. It looked, to Sylvia, as though the corps of engineers had said to themselves, "I will leave my mark here. Behold the power of man, the collective desire of the people." Considering it, she was both impressed and dismayed. The building was not ugly. It was obviously functional; however, man's instinct to control the landscape was all too evident.

For a while they rode over wide, well-packed stretches of sand. To her right the dunes rose thirty or forty feet, much higher than those on Mustang Island, each one topped with a sprinkling of sea oats. A few miles down a wooden sign warned 4 WHEEL DRIVE VEHICLES ONLY. The sun slunk out of its cloud cover.

"Put your hat on," Roy reminded her.

She jammed it down on her head, hating the stiffness of new straw. He'd bought it for her, a cowboy hat with a low crown and wide brim, which, she was afraid, would continually blow off.

"You look like a Texan now." He had been teasing her the past few days about becoming an Easterner. No matter where Ohio really was, it was east to him, inland, an effete place.

He put his own hat on and, wearing it, appeared perfectly normal, not a man playing a part, but a man whose hat was a necessary part of him.

"It's so filthy down here." She waved one hand at all the plastic bottles, pieces of netting, and driftwood strewn in a ragged line.

"High tide washes it up."

"Why don't the rangers—?"

"They can't keep the whole island clean."

The horses picked their feet up higher now in the soft sand. Sometimes there were jeep tracks to follow, but they were often deeply rutted. It was slow going.

"The world's a dirty place," Sylvia said, gazing at a white bleach bottle half covered by tarred net.

Roy shrugged. "Things wash up here."

"If people didn't use the ocean for a garbage can—"

"Some of it can't be helped. Nets get torn and float off. Markers get loose."

All the same, the trash depressed her. The little bits of material like worn-out dishcloths twined around pieces of rusty metal, a broken fishing pole, part of a saucer, the rag-tag ends of everything, each with a previous use, a history of its own, lay at last, useless, forgotten, unclaimed by anyone. Flotsam and jetsam, she repeated the words. All they meant to her was a great sprawling line of debris pushed by furious tides to this desert shore. Arabs or lions . . . either could appear from behind the dunes . . . brown men in white, wind-whipped robes regarded her silently and at their feet tawny lions snarled. Would one watch over her that night as the lion watched Rousseau's gypsy sleeping? So peaceful, so threatening.

Her dream of the lions was broken by two enormous jack rabbits symmetrically balanced in front of two dunes as if they were posing for a travel folder picture. An oil well drilling rig reared between the dunes in the exact middle of the background. Alert ears raised, the rabbits remained in one position while she and Roy plodded by fifty feet away.

Riders Of The Purple Purslane, cover of a cheap western novel, that's what we look like. The cowboy and his sweetheart . . . unreal, too real. Why did I come? Because he asked me. And when it's over, this ride, this last week, I'll go back to Ohio, to green hills, a river, to Franklin. No. I can't live with Franklin after this. Not for the sake of convenience, not for one day.

"Thirsty?"

"A little."

"Go ahead." He unscrewed the top of one of the canteens and handed it to her. "There's no use to hold back. We've got plenty of water."

"The horses . . . Where will they . . . ?" I have not thought of the simplest things. Do I lack even the most basic sense of survival?

"Over there." He gestured toward the dunes. "On the Laguna Madre side. There're wells. I have the ranger's list of them."

If she'd asked Franklin he would have been sure she was accusing him of lack of foresight—"My God, Sissy, don't you know I would have thought of that!"—but Roy never seemed to feel he was being accused of anything. He relied on her absolute trust.

"We're carrying a little for them too . . . just in case. It's a ways between wells."

"What else is over there?"

"Nothing much. Fishing shacks. Washovers. Storms push the water up across the island and then it runs off and sand fills in. Treasure hunters waste a lot of time behind the dunes. I dug around some. You can make more using a metal detector on the beach after the weekend crowd is gone. Fellow I know did that all one summer. I went with him sometimes. He picked up five dollars in change before sunset. Down here you're not supposed to use detectors, but people sneak them in anyways. Treasure nuts. About the poorest people I've ever known. They spend everything they've got for fancy equipment hoping to find something never was theirs."

Sylvia laughed. "Wouldn't anybody like to find a pirate's chest full of doubloons?"

"Anybody might, but that's not what these guys are looking for. Most of them think they'll find gold bars, and if they're around anywhere, it's out there." He nodded toward the sea. "A lot of currents come together. It's known for shipwrecks."

"Right out here?"

"No, more toward Big Shell further on down. About halfway. You ought to hear my old man carry on about it. He knows a lot of shrimpers who've lost their boats down there."

They turned the horses toward a rim of packed sand near the water to make room for a jeep grinding through. Roy waved at the driver as he passed.

"That's Thompson from Corpus. He's out here every weekend bringing somebody to fish or driving tourists. One time right after a hurricane I rode with him. We made it to the Mansfield jetties and back in three hours. We were the only ones on the beach and the sand was packed good. Like he's going now though, it'll take him half a day to get there. It's a hell of a ride."

Sylvia look enviously at the back of Thompson's jeep bumping over a rise. Already sore, she wondered if Thompson's jolts were any worse than the slow-creaking saddle aches she was enduring.

"Where are we now?"

"Little Shell. See how it's all broken up. Lots of sand dollars here usually, and clam shells. Want to get down awhile?"

Hundreds of shell fragments crunched underfoot as she slid off the sorrel. Strange to stand on a beach wearing boots, a long-sleeved shirt, and jeans. So many clothes when she usually had on so few. It felt good to stretch her legs.

"How far down are we?"

"About twenty miles from Bob Hall Pier."

"I don't remember—"

"You didn't see it. It's back there at the park on the other side of the ranger station. We've only ridden about ten or twelve miles. The worst twenty are ahead between here and Big Shell and we got to go inland to a well."

"Oh! Look!" Whole sand dollars lay scattered everywhere on top of bits of shells. Sylvia ran to pick them up. "The boys will love these."

"Where are you going to carry them?"

"Damn! I guess they would break if I rode with them all day today and tomorrow. I've just never seen so many all together."

"The saddle bags will be almost empty by the time we come back. More sand dollars will wash up by tomorrow. Come on. These horses need to tank up. See that road yonder?" He pointed to a faint trail between the dunes. "The Dunn Ranch used to be out here. I know some old men who cowboyed for them. Supposed to be water at a corral in there."

Behind the dunes, cut off from the sea breeze, it was hotter. Grass flats were broken by scattered smaller dunes. Though Sylvia could see the vegetation better, she could identify only the crawling railroad vine, its purple flowers tangled with yellow wild indigo.

"Look, there's a hawk. In the winter sandhill cranes fly down."

"Didn't the Karankawas hunt around here?"

"I don't know. Maybe."

It was the first time she'd asked him anything about the area he couldn't answer. "On the way from Dallas we stopped in a museum in San Antonio. The boys were crazy about the Karankawa canoe, a hollowed log really. I ended up reading all the placards in the exhibit to them. I brought some books on Texas history with me and read parts to Edwin. The only thing he really wants to hear about is Indians." She laughed and plucked at the reins self-consciously. He read little or nothing. Fearful of exposing the great difference in their education, she tried not to talk about books when she was with him.

"I don't remember anybody ever reading to me. It's good you do it. They're bright kids."

"Sometimes I think it doesn't help much. Firsthand experience is better."

"Well, they couldn't be Indians."

Sylvia laughed.

Riding around a low dune they saw a straggling remnant of a wooden corral fence. Roy located a rusty pump at the far side, primed it, and watered both horses from a heavy canvas bag hung on a post. Sylvia sat on a rail watching him.

"It's beautiful back here, wilder than the beach really."

"I don't know if it's any wilder. Most people stay on the beach side."

"What's that over there?" She pointed to a small animal pushing dirt onto a mound.

"Gopher. There's ground squirrels and rats too, only you don't catch sight of them too often."

Sylvia climbed off the rail and, as quietly as she could, walked toward the dune, hoping to see the gopher better. Six feet from him an ominous rattle sounded. Searching the ground wildly, she saw the snake's coiled diamond back clearly marked against the sand. Beautiful and deadly. For an instant she stood paralyzed, then all the warning voices of her childhood gathered in one brief command: "Run!"

"Roy!" She screamed as she ran toward him in spite of telling herself to be quiet.

"Snake," she panted. "Rattler." Each muscle in her body was vibrating. She wanted to go on running down the trail back up the beach to the apartment to solid cement floors.

"Hey. Steady. You've seen rattlers before, haven't you?"

"Not that close." She shuddered, remembering the long pale underside of a dead rattler dangling from a stick held in her father's hand. He'd been out dove hunting, shot the snake, and brought it home to show her. "Look at his rattles. How many are there?" She'd counted six and locked the number in her head until this moment.

"My father killed one once, and I took the boys to see the snakes in the San Antonio Zoo. They were behind glass. It's not anything like coming on one." She shuddered again.

Leaning against him, her own fears calmed, she felt a tremor in his body, an inner shakiness he was trying to hold in rigid control.

"Roy, what is it?"

"I . . . I don't know. Caught your shakes maybe. Come on, let's get the hell out of here."

At the pump Sylvia splashed water on her face as if to wake herself from a bad dream. Roy hung the water bag on his saddle horn. They both mounted and, with some relief, turned their faces toward the sea.

"Will we have to go this far inland for water next time?"

"I'm not sure. About halfway down at the old ranch headquarters we'll have to go in a ways, but at the ranger cabin—it's further on, near the wreck of the *Nicaragua*—we won't have far to go. They've got a tank there big enough to swim in."

They rode on down to Big Shell, an outward curve of the coast in mid-island. Here waves hit the beach with such force that small shells were broken. The largest and heaviest were carried in and even those were often broken or worn away until only central spirals, cores of whelks and conches, or battered halves of scallops remained. Large cockle shells lay intact on top of the fragments. Sylvia pointed them out to Roy. Yes, they would stop here also on their way back.

Just below Big Shell in sight of the upturned keel of a wrecked shrimp boat they camped at noon. Using long pieces of driftwood and collapsible aluminum tent poles, Roy stretched two nylon flies, one for them, one for the horses. They were to rest four hours, then continue after the harsh afternoon sun had lost its force. Riding by moonlight they could reach the Mansfield jetty, camp again till daybreak, then ride back, stopping once more at Big Shell at noon.

Sylvia sank down on a quilt Roy's mother had pieced of tiny squares of printed cotton.

"There's my Sunday shirt when I was fourteen. Here's one of Mother's dresses." He pointed them out with stubby brown fingers. She pulled off her new boots. Bought at the same store where she had gotten the hat, she despised them even more. The only pair they had which would fit her narrow heel had a longhorn steer head inset in red on the tops. Dude boots, cheap souvenirs of Texas a wandering tourist might take home to wear to a costume party. Roy had insisted on them and once they were bought he'd told her she must break them in before the trip. She'd worn them riding every day. Edwin and Richard admired her boots and begged for some of their own until she got them each a pair.

"Mama, I want some with red cows on them!" Edwin had wailed.

Luckily all boots in children's sizes were plain dark brown. Both boys stomped around in them proudly even when they had nothing on but bathing suits. How could she leave them for two whole days and nights Oh, it was wrong! But Anna was good with them . . . patient.

He stood beside her pulling off his shirt. "You'll feel better after you get in the water."

"Now?" Dazed by the sun, she wanted to cool off, yet she was already so exhausted she felt the quilt, like a vast compelling magnet, pulling her down.

"We've ridden the worst of it, gotten over the soft sand. The rest is easy."

Easy! Tiny pinpricks of light exploded behind her closed eyelids. Her legs ached and her seat felt like she'd been riding an ironing board through hell. How could it be easy? They had at least thirty-five miles more to go to the Mansfield Channel and sixty miles to ride back. At her own pace she could have made the trip well in three days. Trying to make it in two was unbearable. She was sick of sun, gritty blowing sand, the continual sway of her body in the saddle, and endless winds pushing in from the sea. Why was she doing it? Why, in God's name, did she think she had to endure this? Because Roy asked . . . I followed. Always following, first Franklin, now Roy. But, I've done this because I wanted to. I can't sit down here in the middle of Padre Island and wail like a child, I wanna go home! Even if I do. Even if the nearest I want to get to a beach again is listening to Debussy's *La Mer.*

Roy sat down beside her and pulled off his boots. "You're tired, I know. Try this." He handed her a canteen.

Lime juice, water, a little sugar. Nothing she'd ever swallowed had tasted so good . . . nectar of the gods . . . ambrosia. No, they ate that. Franklin's mother made a southern version of it for dessert every Christmas. Mrs. Parrish . . . Christmas . . . Franklin. Why am I thinking of these things? Sunstroke?

"I kept my hat on." She looked up at Roy, who was unbuttoning her shirt. "I was afraid of losing it. So sleepy . . . Why am I so—?"

"Sylvia, listen to me!" Urgency grated his voice. "You've got to get in the water and cool off. You could have fever—I thought you were used to the beach."

"Oh, I am. I am. I've never been on the beach so long in my life." She nodded willingly. His worry for her was delicious, she must not let him think anything was his fault though.

"I wanted to come." Digging her elbows in the quilt she pushed herself into a sitting position. The wind fluttered her shirt open, drying her sweaty skin immediately. "Let me get my suit. It's in one of the saddle bags." When she stood up she discovered her legs were wobbly. She held on to Roy's shoulder while he helped her step awkwardly out of her jeans.

"Whew. That's better. Where did you put the bags? Oh, I see."

"You are beautiful, you know."

"If I lose about twenty or thirty more pounds."

"No. You're beautiful right now . . . like you are. If you weren't so feverish, I'd—"

"Here? In the open?"

"Why not?"

"Someone might see us."

He shrugged. "Not many people down here today. I could pile up some more driftwood— No, you've got to get in the water. We'll both go and take the horses." He jerked off his shirt and jeans.

"I stink! I can even smell myself!" Sylvia rubbed her finger under her nose.

"So do I. Something really would be wrong if we didn't."

"Roy, where are your underclothes?"

"Only wear them when visiting ladies."

"You don't usually?"

"No."

Sylvia laughed. "Well, if you're going in naked I can do without this, at least." She threw off her bra and threw it on the heap of clothes.

"And those?" He pointed at her pants.

"I need something between me and the horse."

"No, you don't. Try it. I bet you've never been swimming naked in your life."

"Once when I was a child . . . in a creek somewhere. I don't mind trying, but on horseback . . . somebody really will see us that high up."

"You can slide off and stay in till they're gone. I'll drop some towels near the water for us."

"Oh, all right." She put her thumbs in both sides of her pants and pulled them off. Embarrassed, she looked down to see if her flesh was blushing, then glanced up and saw him watching.

"You want some help?"

"No. I'm not so shaky now. I feel silly."

"When I take your clothes off you don't mind."

"When you undress me . . . that's different. We're making love."

"We're making love now. I guess I wanted to see you naked in the daylight." She endured his look for a long moment, realizing every fault he could see, the stretch marks of pregnancy, the sag of her belly, her swollen breasts. These flaws she knew so well washed out of her mind under his gaze. It was her body and he liked it.

He turned to get the horses. Sylvia stepped out of the circles of nylon around each ankle as though freed from hobbles and followed him, a chill rippling down her back. Was it only the strangeness of being totally nude on a beach at high noon, or was she a little feverish?

Roy made a stirrup of his hands and boosted her up on the sorrel. Extremely conscious of the horse's backbone between her thighs, she wondered if Lady Godiva was given a saddle. The image of Lady Godiva covered by her long hair riding through a wintery medieval town filled with absolutely moral people who refused to peep opposed to her view of herself still overweight, only her head covered by short curls, was so incongruous she started giggling aloud.

"What is it?" Roy, in the lead, checked his horse and looked back.

"Me and Lady Godiva! Next time I'll bring a long wig."

"You and Lady who?"

"Never mind."

He held out his hand and she took it.

"The horses may be a little spooky here. It gets deeper quicker."

"What do we do?"

"Roll off, but hold onto the reins. OK?"

She nodded.

Kicking the horses' sides with their bare heels, they rode straight into the waves. Roy's bay went in more willingly. Sylvia was soon stranded in water up to her knees.

He shouted. "Throw me the reins. I'll lead him in further."

When he turned his horse to come toward her, the bay lost his footing. Holding on to the reins, she slipped off the sorrel to swim to him.

"Current!" He called over the noise of waves breaking, but to her he seemed to be shouting, "Come on!" The sorrel, swimming now, followed her lead. Where was Roy? Had he been washed off or had he— There was the bay swimming toward shore. Every wave was mountainous. "Roy!" She began shouting. The sorrel, lunging toward shore, wrenched the reins loose. She was caught up by a wave and sucked under again and again. Holding what little breath she had left, she thrashed wildly to the surface. For minutes, she felt, she lost consciousness. There was nothing, then a roaring devouring sound, then nothing. I . . . I . . . I. Pieces of shells rattled past her.

On her knees she breathed, coughing, vomiting salt water; she collapsed, her naked body a white speck of flesh sprawled on the sand.

"You all right?"

Roy's hand on her shoulder. She struggled to her knees.

"I knew it was deeper here. Didn't know how much. The current— A rip tide. We were lucky. I was afraid—"

Sylvia, barely hearing him, nodded. She stared down at grains of sand magnified, sparkling, whole. It was there, the earth, life, herself. Tears fell off her cheeks. More saltwater for the sea. Useless gratitude. All I've got.

Roy held out his hand to her. She ignored it. Slowly lifting herself she got to her feet and walked back up the beach to get the towels dropped at the water's edge.

"I didn't know—" He began again.

Stopping abruptly, she faced him. "It's not your fault. It's mine."

"It was my idea."

"Yes." She could concede that. "Of course it was, but I didn't have to—" She handed him one towel, wrapped another around herself. "I didn't have to come."

In the shade under the fly Sylvia asked for fresh water, wet the towel, and sponged salt off her skin mechanically as if she were bathing one of her own children. They pulled their clothes on again.

"The horses?"

"Probably grazing behind the dunes. I can catch them later."

"I have to go back." Let him think I mean all the way to Cincinnati, to Franklin. It's easier for him, will hurt him less, let him believe I'm being a dutiful wife, a careful mother. I'll probably have to be there for divorce proceedings anyway.

"I figured you would. Thompson will be driving by sometime this afternoon. He'll take you."

"I'm sorry." She touched his arm where the sleeve of his shirt was rolled back.

"It don't matter."

Worn down to calmness, they sat on the quilt cross-legged facing each other, eating sandwiches she had made and he had packed in the saddle bags. Slowly they passed the canteen of lime water back and forth, sharing equitably as two friendly strangers meeting by chance at the same campsite might divide and share supplies.